TIME FOR A

KILLING

He was a somber and a deadly-looking figure when he rode into town. Johnny Velantry was a tall man, restless-eyed and quiet—a man who had spent a hard life wandering up and down the West looking for a half-forgotten face . . .

He was standing at the bar when Big Red Kincaid came in at the head of his men. Then Johnny knew the long hunt was over. It was time for a killing.

CAST OF
CHARACTERS

JOHN VELANTRY never told anyone what he was hunting. But he knew that either he or Kincaid would die when he found it.

BIG RED KINCAID had torn an empire from the lawless territory. He didn't intend to have it taken from him.

COPPER ANN KINCAID knew her father was right until Johnny Velantry came to town. Then things began to look different.

BEN ALVERSON had waited a long time for Kincaid's daughter. No man could cut him out and live.

STELLA ADAMS didn't care what Big Red had done. She was his whenever he wanted.

FRANK DAUNCE
SEASTRON DAUNCE } came up the trail from Texas with a hard case crew. They threw in with Velantry.

West of ABILENE

BY VINGIE ROE

WILDSIDE PRESS

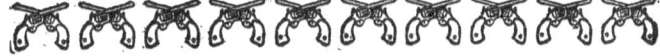

TO MY BELOVED FRIEND
IDA LOUISE MOORE
THIS BOOK IS AFFECTIONATELY INSCRIBED

Chapter One

IT WAS AFTERNOON OF A WARM SPRING DAY AND THE CATTLE town, roaring through the night, sleeping soddenly in the middle hours, was waking up.

Sprinkling can and broom wet down and dusted off the raw plank platforms, the wide steps before the equally raw plank buildings—saloon and gambling hall and store, hotel and more saloons. Saddled horses switched impatiently at the flies; wagon and buckboard, cart and high-top buggy crowded for place at the stout peeled-sapling hitch rails that adorned the length of the wide main street. On the fringes of the young metropolis, that prideful thing, the home, was rubbing elbows with the traditional and purely male prerogatives of the cow town.

"'S a dam' shame," a man in dirty fringed buckskins, leaning on the rail in front of the Lone Star Palace, said pensively, "how soft this here place is a-gettin'. W'y, I mind me, an' 'tain't a mite over six year back, when they wa'n't a petticoat, barrin' a certain kind, this side Dodge City. An' now look. Th' whole country's crawlin' with wimmen."

"Well, Sam," his companion, equally soiled, equally pensive after the hard night just past, said judicially, "that there's progress. 'Twarn't for women there wouldn't be no men. An' that's an appallin' thought. Yes, sir. Appallin'! First time it ever struck me, too. But where'd we be—me, you, ever'body—if there hadn't of ben a woman som'ers in th' background? You just tell me that an' mind yore manners hereinafter."

Sam Bolin straightened up, as well as was possible under the circumstances, and regarded the speaker in admiring

1

astonishment. "You're dam' right," he said handsomely, "an' I apologize. Shake." They shook solemnly and as solemnly re-entered the Lone Star. So profound a truth called for libations to honor its discovery.

The Lone Star Palace was something to look at, something of pride and a certain awe to its humbler patrons, of pride minus the awe to those others who stood in awe of nothing. These were the cattlemen, the early day tycoons, who lived in the wide, sparsely settled country and ran it with highhanded arrogance. Easy, rugged, sure of themselves and their own private world, they wagered fortunes on horn and hoof and sometimes trebled them in a single year, sometimes were wiped out to the last hide. But riding the wave or swamped in its undertow, they were a breed to themselves and no man's weaklings. They roistered, drank, and whored with a lust that took no thought to anything beyond the day, the night, the place. They had a code of their own with its high points and its shady ones and, good or bad, they were all tarred with the same stick. Many a man among them, starting his fall drive with a modest herd, arrived at railhead with one vastly augmented along the way, and no one asked or looked a question. But in their wake there were often deserted buildings of this or that small home ranch, the lonely barn doors swinging in the wind, the woman's garden dying in its paled-in place. Beyond Dodge City and Abilene, to west-southwest, there was a latitude so vast that only the strong survived in it.

Now, on this Saturday afternoon, a sizable sprinkling of these gentry was trickling into their favorite stamping ground, the Lone Star Palace saloon and gambling hall. Young and old and middle-aged, they foregathered for the weekly jamboree which roared through the town for forty-eight hours and left it at their end drained and still and drab, like a woman of the streets too old for her trade.

The Lone Star was ready for them. It had been cleaned and burnished in the early hours of the new day, its long bar polished, its glasses shining on the ancient walnut bar-back beneath the monstrous mirror in its wide gold frame. The floor had been freshly sanded, the brass spittoons scrubbed with the same substance, as had the foot rail which ran the bar's length. The fixtures of the Palace were part of that pride in the place which its patrons felt so strongly.

"Ain't another lookin' glass this side Boston can hold a candle to it," they said offhandedly, "and's for th' bar itself, they do say Jean Lafitte took it off a captured English brig that was bringin' it to New Orleans for some high-falutin' Spanish Creole. Yes, sir." And the speaker would run a hand lovingly along the rounded edge where the deep patina of uncounted like caresses had left their ageless mark.

There was, too, something more than civic pride in the lingering touches which these men of a wild frontier laid on the lovely wood. This was something secret and senti-mental, a vicarious contact with a presence so desirable and unattainable that there was no other method of personal approach. Many a calloused palm, laid so, tingled at thought of that one which had preceded it, would follow it again.

As the warm day drowsed toward midafternoon, the place began to fill more rapidly. Men in every conceivable manner of garb stamped up the hollow steps outside, across the plank porch, in at the wide-open doors. Men in jeans and calico shirts, vests and "sleeve-histers," their broad hats cocked on their heads if they were young, more soberly worn if they were not, their feet in worn boots, the loose spurs jingling. These were the cattlemen, owner and rider alike, and they were far in the majority, of an undisputed importance.

There were settlers, too, a quieter, more modest type who

accepted their obvious unpopularity with the dogged tenacity of men who know their rights and stand upon them. For that they were disliked, held in open contempt, there was no doubt. This was cattle country in its earliest, most lawless, and flamboyant period, and as such it resented any change, any encroachment. And the homesteaders foreshadowed change and encroachment with a tragic surety which was not yet fully felt or understood by the beef barons. They merely overlooked the few nesters who had filtered in with their usually shabby wagons and household gear, waited for them to starve out and pass away as any other shadow on the land passed, like drought or murrain among the stock.

The grass was limitless and abundant. The Chisholm Trail came up from Texas to end at Abilene, the raw new town at railhead. A future yet unvisioned promised exciting things, and they had their town—and the Lone Star Palace. What more could men in their reasonable senses desire?

Men from the widely scattered ranches; drifters up from the Llano Estacado, that almost uncharted sea of grass and rolling plain, like Sam Bolin—they drank and gambled and did other things less aboveboard which took their scant money. Taken by and large it was a motley crowd which moiled in the Lone Star, a fair cross-section of the time and place.

Curly Bates behind the bar, an imposing figure with the black hair parted meticulously in the middle of his head and plastered into two elegant rings above his eyebrows, flicked a last imagined bit of dust from the shining dark surface before him and smiled at the line that was beginning to form along the foot rail.

"Well, gents," he said affably, "what'll it be? Name your poison."

They named it, drank, and drifted over to the tables to begin their entertainment, each to his choice; poker, vingt-et-un, Mexican monte, faro.

The faro layout and a roulette wheel occupied the center of the wide floor, aristocrats of chance among the less spectacular games, and here the tycoons gathered as if by common consent. The riders played poker for the most part, that solid stand-by of the West; and scouts, drifters, and riflemen gravitated naturally toward the monte table. Monte, the easy, the familiar, played on a blanket beside a lone campfire or on the brushed-off earth itself by half-breed, Mexican, and white alike—it was the comfortable partner of a thousand trails, the lowly mistress of the indigent.

In the colorful crowd that already nearly filled the room two men stood out with a nameless but positive distinction. One of these was Ben Alverson, owner of the best string of freight wagons hauling out of Abilene. He stood at the bar, one elbow crooked back upon it, the heel of his boot hooked over the foot rail below, his wide hat tilted over his right temple, his cool eyes covering the scene before him. He did not drink and he rarely gambled, yet no man there would have called him soft. They knew better.

The other was a stranger. Tall, dark, quiet, he wore the garb of the professional gambler commonly accepted throughout the loose frontier as the earmark of that peculiar gentry. This consisted of a wide black hat, white shirt, black tie, a handsome black coat whose elegantly cut skirts reached nearly to his knees, black trousers worn outside the polished, soft, black boots. Taken altogether he was a striking figure in any setting. His hair and eyes were black, too, but the skin of his face and hands was not of the traditional paleness usually associated with a man of the indoors, the lamps, the night. It was the one false note in the character otherwise so plainly stamped upon him.

But true to his type as the needle to the pole, he had taken a glass of whiskey straight and gone directly to the roulette table. Aristocrat of games, aristocrat of players, they complemented each other perfectly.

And all over the place the eyes of men appraised him, silently, with a bafflement that was foreign to their usual quick decision.

He was too elegant and too brown.

They had seen him come into town two hours back riding a horse which had drawn their interest like a magnet. A tall horse, slim and graceful on its hard and slender legs, short-coupled, high of head and arching neck even though the dust of many miles was on its sweated coat. It was dark as a glossy chestnut with something of its depth and faint, suggested gold. A handsome creature, quick and quiet, with something about it of the quality of a bent bow, taut and ready. It had carried a strange saddle, too, low of horn and cantle, short of skirt, and of far lighter weight than anything seen in the cow country. Behind the saddle there had been a roll, made up, no doubt, of the master's sole possessions, since there was nothing else to hold them. The man had stopped at the Blue Top Hotel, dropped his rein over the hitch rail, gone in and engaged a room, and come directly out again to take the horse around back to the stable, where he proceeded to rub and curry the animal, to feed it carefully, before he cared for himself.

"Must think a heap of th' critter," an observer opined. "An' at that it ain't no ordinary one. Wonder where it come from?"

"From fur," another said. "It's lean but it ain't pore. It's got on good iron shoes, but they're wore pretty thin. Ben reset, I bet, a many times."

So the handsome clothes, a little wrinkled from their compression in the slender roll, had replaced the calico shirt, the denim jeans of the stranger's arrival, and here he was all ready for the coming night, the drink, the cards, the roulette wheel, the slowly rising excitement of the time and place.

The sense of this rising was an almost tangible thing,

something that began to come with the slanting sun outside, that grew with every step upon the sounding porch,
that filled the gambling hall with a tension, a waiting, a listening that was apparent on men's faces.

The Lone Star Palace was prepared and starting on its
night of revelry, yet there was something lacking. It was
like a swimmer touching foot to water, yet halting on the
bank, not quite ready for the full, engulfing plunge.

And suddenly someone raised his head, another moved
on booted feet, a third pushed back a chair noiselessly on
the sanded floor, for what they waited for was in the wind.
It was a sound, faint and far at first, but rising steadily as
the tension in the room had risen, and it was beautiful to
hear. It was the sound of hoofs, ringing on the sounding
board of the prairie like the beat of distant drums, as timed,
precise, and musical. Two horses, rocking in from the out-
skirts of the town in that most beautiful of all gaits, the
natural, untrained single-foot. Tap, strike, strike, tap—perfectly syncopated, square and balanced, it sent a thrill of
pure delight into the heart of every man in the room who
knew horses, and few there were in the time and place
who didn't.

And it seemed to hit with the sharpest impact of all on
the consciousness of that newcomer in the long black coat
who had settled himself at the roulette table. His hand,
rising to push his hat a little back from his forehead, was
arrested in the motion. It remained so, held up in a mean-
ingless gesture, the graceful brown fingers curved and
parted. But no one noticed him or his reaction, for the peak
of the late day was here, the thing for which the Lone Star
had been waiting.

The look of excitement deepened in men's faces, the
shine of anticipated pleasure was in their eyes.

For those were Kincaid horses, the horses of the Fingermarks, and there were no others like them in the country,

perhaps in all the world, so far as any knew. They were the treasures of the Kincaid brand, its prides and its hostages, so ironbound guarded that they were never left alone. And with them came, undoubtedly, the most spectacular two people north of the Rio Grande.

Chapter Two

THE ROCKING DRUM ROLL HEIGHTENED IN TEMPO AND VOLUME to roar up to the hitch rail in front and come suddenly to an abrupt, split-second stop, as effortless and smooth as the sudden falling of a gust of wind.

There were steps on the planks outside, a shadow in the open door, and a woman stood there. A girl rather, a slim tall stripling of a girl, lance-straight, lance-proud, her eager face so lighted with the zest of life that it seemed to glow. She wore a dark green riding habit, its plain, tight-fitting, long-sleeved basque buttoned straight down from chin to hipline, its instep-length skirt lifted a little by the loop over her right wrist. She wore no hat and she needed none, for the tightly wound braids of her hair covered her little head like a shining cap, fringed at brow and temple and nape of neck by the small short curls that lay there. It was this hair, with its amazing color, weight, and texture, which gave her her nickname from railhead to the southern end of the Chisholm Trail.

For this was Copper Ann Kincaid.

And just behind her, like a monstrous shield and buckler, stood her father, Big Red Kincaid, his wild blue eyes already laughing at the scene before him, his great red beard still parted down his breast from the wind of his ride.

Prideful, arrogant, the surest of any in their certain-sure breed, they stood for a moment in the square of the doorway with the summer sky behind them, and it was easily apparent why the room had waited for them.

Then Big Red waved a hand above the girl's head, a gesture which took in largely every man in the place.

9

"Hello, boys!" he boomed, in a voice which matched his huge body.

"Howdy, Red!" the room called back in chorus. "Afternoon, Miss Ann!"

"Hello," she answered in a clear, carrying voice. "Room for two more?"

"For you? Say!" someone cried on a note of wondering joy, "you can have th' whole dam' place an' every one that's in it!"

Ann Kincaid tipped back her handsome head at that and laughed with keen relish. "I might believe you, Sandy," she said, "if I didn't know you're lying! How about that girl over on Big Bend?"

"Well," the rider said a trifle sheepishly, "if a feller can't have th' moon, he's got to be satisfied with stars."

"And how do you think that girl will like that speech, if she ever hears of it?" Ann shot back.

"She ain't goin' to hear it," the boy said grinning. "An' if she does I still contend it's justified."

Ann laughed again. She was pulling off the fine kid gauntlet gloves she always wore, her long blue eyes traveling swiftly over every inch of the big room, every man in it. In that flashing and comprehensive glance they rested for a moment on the black-clad stranger at the roulette table. In that quick space of time she knew exactly what he looked like, the color of his eyes and hair and skin, the cut of his good clothes. It was a trick she had from Big Red himself, that swift and accurate appraisal.

"Can't tell when you'll have th' need to remember a man or a place," he sometimes said, "an' know you're right."

The girl slapped the gloves together in her left palm and laid them on the end of the bar. Then, with her hand laid on that polished edge in a gesture almost loving in its keen appreciation of beauty wherever found, she walked slowly down along its length toward where the freighter, Ben Alverson, had lounged. He was not lounging now.

With the first sight of her in the doorway he had straightened and turned toward her, his hat off, his lean face sober, his hungry eyes on her copper-colored braids.

Every man in the room was conscious of that smooth, caressing slide of her hand along the bar. It was what made them touch it themselves with a replica of that caress. It was the closest most of them would ever get to Copper Ann Kincaid. And the stranger at the roulette table, hat off also, watched her with an odd expression on his face. It was not the first time he'd seen a woman in a barroom. It was the first time he'd seen one like her there.

"Hello, Ben," Ann said civilly. "Watching your drivers so they won't get into trouble?"

"Hello, Ann," Alverson answered. "Not exactly."

The girl grinned like a boy. "Just sampling a few fleshpots yourself, maybe?"

The man flushed to the temples where two iron-gray wings spread back along his dark hair. His abstemiousness was well-known, and this was a sly little thrust which she was not above giving when the opportunity arose, though she took its sting away in the same moment with the light touch she gave his arm in passing.

She went direct to the poker tables, seated herself in one of the chairs offered her, and smiled around at the flattered group.

"Button your shirts, boys," she said. "I feel so lucky today I'm likely to win them all right off your backs."

They dealt her in as though she were a man, and the game proceeded, its tempo stepped up excitedly. This was common procedure, for Ann Kincaid was a good gambler and loved it with a lively ardor. That she was the only woman in a room full of frontier men was nothing strange, for Big Red owned the Lone Star Palace, as he owned the Blue Top Hotel, one of the two general stores, and the only blacksmith shop. In fact, he very nearly owned the town, and his daughter was free of it all. That he and his riders were always behind her was a guarantee of safety and decorum which no man in his senses would forget for a moment. The girl was an institution, and Kincaid and his outfit were a bigger one.

But if they ruled the fenceless prairies and the roaring gambling halls, the matter ended there. The women of the town were another matter. When Ann came rocking in along the dusty street in her prim green habit, on the finest sidesaddle west of the Mississippi and handling the big blue stallion, Stormwind, like the expert horsewoman she was, hostile eyes looked from behind lace curtains, soft lips hardened into condemning lines.

"Look at her!" they told each other over back fences. "Foregathering with men like any open hussy! More so! Even Stella Adams shows more modesty in public!"

And many a teen-age daughter got her young ears roundly boxed for following the shining coppery head and flowing habit with envious and admiring eyes.

If Ann Kincaid knew of this she gave little sign, either to the outside world or to herself. In fact, she did know of it to a certain extent, and it afforded her an immense secret amusement. More than that, it added fuel to the flame of inordinate vanity which burned in her at all times, for she was the vainest woman on the whole frontier. Vain of her beauty; her skin of creamy gold; her long hands, always so white and soft from the protecting gloves but the most deceptive thing about her, for they held the strength of a man. Vain of her long blue eyes, the rich brown lashes and straight brows above them. But mostly she was vain of her hair. That amazing copper glory, which drew the eyes of men as a magnet draws steel, was to her a sign-manual of her power.

Now she sat in her chair at the canvas-covered table and played like a veteran—a prim, straight figure, elegant in her handsome riding habit, her small feet in their fine leather boots close together. She played good poker, taken by and large, neither too careful nor with much reckless plunging, though she had been known to clean a crowd in record time once in a while. Big Red Kincaid paid little attention to her once she was settled, for he was a confirmed devotee of Mexican monte and never left the game throughout an evening.

The commonest game in the establishment, it put a finger on the man himself, like a signboard pointing to something in him more than ordinarily earthy.

Scattered about the room were seven of his men, Kincaid riders, while two others smoked and lounged outside where Stormwind and Big Red's own special mare, Streaker, waited in hip-dropped rest beside the rail.

For an hour these two men would stand about lazily, to be relieved by two others who had had their turn inside. This was a hard and fast custom of the outfit, for no horse of the Fingermarks was ever left alone away from its own home ranch. And these two were the top of their breed. Built like the steeds of ancient legend, those "drinkers of the wind" whom man has loved and treasured from ages past, they were full brother and sister, out of old Thunderfoot by a prairie stud, and they were the chief possessions of the Kincaid ranch, which was rich in possessions, considered by the standards of the country.

Seventeen full hands at the crest of their withers, short-coupled, broad of haunch and heel and breast, long of high-arched neck and flank and leg above hock and knee, deep-barreled to house their mighty hearts, they were something for all men to marvel at. Their tails were a flowing vanity behind them; their manes flew in the wind like shining banners. Their eyes were large and full and brilliant as winter stars, blue as summer skies. And they were as alike as two peas but for their color. Both roans, that minute flecking of white upon a solid color, the mare was a strawberry pink, the stud a silver blue, and they bore one thing in common which set them apart from all the world.

This was the sign of the Fingermarks, four sharp hori-

zontal stripes inside their knees and hocks which looked
exactly as if a tarry hand had slapped them smartly.

The horses of the Fingermarks. Kincaid horses. More
precious than Big Red's herds of longhorned cattle. Priceless. Above price because there was no standard against
which to measure them.

So their watchers smoked and lounged and talked in low
voices, and the hum of the Lone Star Palace was subdued,
decorous, because a red-haired woman cast the spell of her
presence on it. It had not yet begun to roar. That would
come later, when the sun had gone behind the vast and
distant bulk of the Continental Divide, and Copper Ann
Kincaid had gone racing out of town toward the edgeless
stretches of the Double K ranch.

Big Red lost heavily at monte and roundly cursed the
game and its originators, but Ann was cleaning up after a
modest fashion.

Smiling, calm, she played her cards close to her breast
and one by one she finished off the others, who rose and
threw in their hands.

"It's just no use," Alverson, the freighter, said resignedly.
"A man might as well give up first as last when Copper Ann
sits in a game."

The girl looked up and laughed, gathering her winnings
to the table's edge with a practiced hand.

"I told you," she said. "Gave you fair warning, didn't I?"

"You sure did, Miss Kincaid," he answered handsomely.
"I mean that you not only have the luck of the lovely, but
you're a damn—excuse me—good poker player."

"You bet your boots I am, Ben," she said. "Both lucky
and good." She laid her hands, palms down, on the table
and looked around at the dwindled group. "Looks like I'll
have to quit," she said, "whether I want to or not. I'd hate
to break you all."

Alverson spread his hands, shrugged his heavy shoulders.

He was a big man, easy and slow, with a panther's flowing grace in every muscle, even though the lines of middle age showed in his face, a pair of silver wings stood out along his temples. He had just lost the price of a hundred cows to her. Now he sat down again.

"I never quit, Ann," he said quietly, "if there's reason not to. A lady's wish is that."

"Ha!" Ann said, "I bet——"

What she would have bet was not made known, for there was a step behind her and a soft voice said pleasantly, "May I come in?"

She looked up into quiet dark eyes under black brows and hair, and a flame lighted suddenly in her face, an excitement, an expectation.

"Open game," she said. "Of course."

The man sat down in one of the vacant chairs, picked up the pack of cards and spread them, flicked them together, stacked them expertly, and pushed them forward for the deal to be decided. As no one touched them, Ann took them and dealt one card around, face up. The stranger got the highest card, a jack of hearts, and she pushed the pack back to him.

He took it, cradled it in his left hand, and looked directly at her.

"Straight, stud, or draw?" he asked politely.

"Draw," she answered. "Always."

"Limit?"

"None."

He slid the cards for the cut, dealt them swiftly. Alverson, age man, had already anted the blind, a cowboy beyond him went in, Ann followed, and two cattlemen from Big Bend did likewise. One lone player threw down his hand, and the game started. Alverson drew two cards, the cowboy three, and Ann one. The other two men drew two each, but the dealer threw down his entire hand and drew five new cards.

One look at his filled hand and the cowboy cast in also and left the table. This left Ann with the first say, and she pushed in a stack of chips so high that both men at her left withdrew. The stranger saw and stayed, Alverson saw and raised, the girl covered, the stranger pushed forward all the chips which he had bought, and both Alverson and Ann, after a long look at him, threw down their cards. The man laid down his own, face down, and smiled.

"You win, Mister," Ann Kincaid said easily, "but the day is young."

"Not so very, Ann," Alverson said, glancing toward the open doorway where the light had softened perceptibly, "and Big Red's about ready to kick the table apart over there from the sound of things."

"I guess his luck don't hold," she said. "Bet he——"

Once more she was stopped in what she would have bet, for there was something happening in the street beyond the high plank porch. A confusion of voices suddenly raised in the open street, a thin, high screech which penetrated into the humming sound of the big room at its business.

"Hey! Get away from here!" a man said loudly. "Go on! Get!"

"You get away!" the thin voice said. "Get away from that rail if you don't want a bullet in yer guts! I ain't aimin' to kill a man. Just somethin' a man values. Like I valued what I had oncet. A herd of cattle, that's what I had. An' what I got now? Empty range an' a hungry wife an' kids! I warn yuh! Get away from there. For so help me I'm goin' to kill them two fancy horses what Big Red fancies. Like I fancied them cows he druv——"

Bedlam broke where Big Red Kincaid jumped from his chair and made a rush for the door, his great body slamming over chairs, his boots thundering on the sanded floor. He struck the opening on the run, slid across the porch, and landed in the dust of the street. In a split second he had pulled the gun on his thigh and fired point-blank at the ragged man who stood across the way with an ancient rifle drawing a bead on the ribs of the stallion, Stormwind, the two riders standing in petrified helplessness a little way to the left. Red Kincaid was a famous shot, and the man went down like a rag in a breeze, crumbling at the knees, his shoulders sagging forward, his unkempt head, freed from its tattered hat, rolling backward, his face turned to the high blue sky where the lavender of coming twilight was beginning to edge the drifting, soft, white clouds.

After the turmoil, the cracking shot, a silence fell, thick and smothering and tangible. No one moved or spoke or even seemed to breathe while the pitiful, stark tragedy etched itself indelibly on the minds of the beholders. And then a sigh, so deep, so heavy, so plainly audible that it cut the silence like a blade, came from the open lips of the girl in the green riding habit where she stood on the top step of porch stairs.

"Oh, Red!" she cried, with the sound of tears in her clear voice. "Oh, Red! Did you have to?"

Even in the heart of that stark moment her father heard her, turned his furious face up toward her. To no other living soul would this man have made justification. It was important—imperative, rather—that he do so to her.

"Have to?" he said, in his great voice that carried all down the street and made justification, inadvertently, to all others also. "Of course I had to! Didn't you hear him threaten to kill Sloan and Carter here? A crazy man loose in th' street with a gun! Gone plumb loco! Ready to shoot anyone got in his way. What you mean, girl, have to?"

But Ann Kincaid closed her pale lips and shook her head and fumbled with the gloves which someone gave her. She pulled at the leather helplessly, as if it typified a ruthlessness, a way of life, that shocked her to her foundations, even though she had known it from childhood up.

She did not know that it was the man in the good black clothes who had thrust the gloves against her hand, a branch to the drowning, as it were, a bit to clamp her teeth against. But one man knew it, even in that surcharged moment. Ben Alverson, the freighter, saw the small byplay, and a tide of hot resentment flowed in him. Ann Kincaid—Copper Ann Kincaid—belonged to this place, this town, this country, and the people in it, and no outlander had a right to touch her or to offer her so much as a breath of comfort in distress. Who was he, anyway? Where had he come from? How dared he thrust himself upon her notice?

Ann came blindly down the steps, and her face was working like that of a child on the verge of bitter weeping who tries to hold it back. She went to Stormwind, reached up for rein and saddle horn, and waited to be lifted up. But Big Red, whose sole prerogative it was to hold down his big hand for his daughter's foot and toss her up the stallion's side, for once stood where he was, his smoking gun in loose fingers, and made no move to help her. It was Ennis Sloan who ducked under the rail and did it for him. He handed her the reins and, in the awkward silence which followed her father's words, she swung away and headed out of town.

This time she did not go as she always did, in a flashing run, prideful and spectacular and arrogant because the tide of joyful life was so high in her she could not resist its exploitation; but slowly, with the big horse fretting at the bit. The two riders who had been a part of the painful and dangerous scene, just past, mounted and rode after her. Someone always followed her, and for some reason these two, who had had no chance at the town and its fleshpots, had lost their taste for them. They both had seen her withheld tears.

Others had seen them, too, and almost to a man they wondered silently about their source. For which man, and why? For the dead man in the dust, his wrongs and sorrows nullified? Or for the scowling giant who stood by the saloon's porch with blood on his hands?

No one knew or could venture an opinion. The girl was a law to herself and to every man who laid eyes on her, accepted and adored from respectful distance, not to be questioned. But no one had ever seen her without the flame and fire of her sparkling spirit, the music of her laughter. So it was a sober lot who presently broke up and began to trickle away about the interrupted business of the coming night, and it was a strange thing that few re-entered the Lone Star Palace. For the most part they tramped through the dust to the other saloons—the Double K, the Silver Tip, or Bill Macy's Odeon.

For the first time in his life Big Red Kincaid began to find himself in a widening space of solitude with only the men of his own outfit around him. He had been scowling at the body of the man whose life he had just snuffed out, but now he suddenly raised his head and looked about him. His mouth slowly opened in the midst of his beard, and a vast astonishment spread over his heavy features.

For a moment he stood watching the men in the unusually quiet street, before the full tide of his rising anger engulfed him. When it did he turned so dark it seemed his face must burst from its own congestion.

"Well, I'll be double damned!" he said, in an oddly thick voice. "I'll just be damned!"

Then he slammed the gun in its holster, brushed the wide hat from his head in a forehead-sweeping gesture, and shook his huge shoulders back as if he shook off the world and all it contained. He too was a law, and its arrogance swung back around him like a cloak. He stuck his thumbs in his studded leather belt and strode down the dusty road after the walking men.

Someone stepped off the low porch of the barber shop across the way, several others joined him, and together they picked up the limp heap of shabby clothes and inert flesh

that had been a living man so short a time ago and carried
it into the back room of the raw pine shack and laid it out
on the dirty floor. Another man followed the silent small
cortege and stood looking down upon the dead man. This
was the black-clad stranger.

"Who was he?" he asked presently.

"It's Bill Smith," the barber said. "Used to have a little
spread over across the Little Willow Creek."

"Used to have?"

"Yeah," the other answered shortly.

"Didn't he say something about a wife and kids?"

Hilmer, the barber, straightened up and looked at the
speaker coldly. "Mister," he said pointedly, "you had a
right to hear as much as anyone else."

"Yeah," the gambler said quietly. "Yes, I guess I did."

Then he turned and went out of the place.

The soft, warm, late-spring day was done. The sun was
down behind the distant Rockies, but all the blues and
lavenders and dusky pinks of a prairie twilight were sifting
down upon the lonely, wide-spread world of a sparsely
peopled land. Along the southern edge of the town a little
nameless creek flowed sluggishly beneath its fringe of willows and tall sycamores and elms. Here and there a building
stood, small frame structures of this and that unimportant
enterprise, with vacant spaces between them where the
grass grew raggedly. A path skirted the edge of the street
with the usual hitch rails along it; and here, in the coming
twilight, a woman walked slowly, tentatively, as if she chose
this less frequented side of the main way for reasons of
inconspicuousness.

She was a tall woman, beautifully built, deep-bosomed,
with a still, shut sort of face, and she walked with an as-
surance that was oddly self-effacing. It seemed to say that
she had chosen a way of life in which she had been all
things to all men, yet was withdrawn from life itself, after
a fashion. That she walked here for a purpose was apparent,

too, for her large dark eyes took in the whole small world about and appraised it all. She had heard the shot a little while back, but she had missed its tragic consequences, having come across the little bridge in the willows a bit too late. This was Stella Adams, and she lived in a neat log cabin hidden in trees and underbrush across the creek. Stella Adams, whom all the women of the town hated and feared.

Now as she passed east along the shadowed path she saw the half-savage figure of Big Red Kincaid coming toward her on the other side of the street in that towering rage which held him. She stopped and watched him with such a piercing look it seemed to touch him like a hand, and the man shook his head, slowed in his headlong gait, and glanced about him. His hot blue eyes met her tranquil dark ones, and something passed between them as tangible as speech. It was a call and a promise, and Big Red tossed the hair back from his sweated temples and closed his open mouth.

Stella Adams went swinging on along the path, and Red Kincaid went up the steps to the Double K Saloon. Within the hour all tension in the town had eased, and the place was roaring at its best. Everywhere men, thinking the matter over, had decided Red was well within his rights. Bill Smith was armed, wasn't he? Threatened Sloan and Carter, didn't he? Well, what's a man to do in such a case? Red was right. Shore, he was right! And men slapped his shoulders, told him what a quick thinker he was, how sure his gun hand.

So the anger died in him and his booming laughter filled the Double K, and he began to get drunker than he'd been in seven months. Not since he'd driven the fall beef into Abilene. There was excitement in him, too, gendered by that look he'd had from Stella Adams and slowly mounting as the hours passed. Big Red Kincaid was fifty-four years old, but he was more virile than half the younger men of

the hard-riding, perforce abstemious country. He could
keep a stern rein on himself, but when he let it go he could
raise more hell than anyone. He was letting go tonight. He
was at a peak not all men reach, even once in their lives.
He had killed a man, he had all the liquor he could drink,
and there waited in the cabin in the willows a woman
whose like he had never known any place, any time.

So the town roared and Big Red Kincaid roared with it,
loudest, wildest, strongest of them all.

There was one man, riding quietly across the grassy plain
toward Little Willow Creek, who knew the killer had not
been right. That he had not shot in defense of human life,
the lives of his two riders, but to save his big blue stallion.
The half-crazed, ragged, erstwhile cattleman with the rifle
had not been gunning for men. He had plainly said so,
warned them to step out of range. Everyone had heard him.
Even the girl had heard him. Yet no one had brought up
the fact.

Big Red was an institution. Big Red was immune. And
yet, as by common consent, the men had moved away from
him in the first shock of the happening. But this was a loose
frontier, a lawless land for the most part, and killings were a
common thing. West of the Chisholm Trail there was
little place for the weak, for those who could not take and
hold what they took.

So the rider on the chestnut horse went into the soft
dark night, his hands folded on his pommel, his hat low
on his right temple, and thought long thoughts of his own.
These had to do with a time and place far distant from
these, with old sorrow and an ancient pain, and with a
cold hard thing that lived where his heart should have
been.

But he thought, too, of the long white hands of a woman
on a gaming table, of the light behind her shining head,
and lastly of unshed tears in her blue eyes. He had seen

many women in his fairly short life, but none like this one. However, he was a womanless man. There was in his plan of existence no place for them. So he took his mind from Ann Kincaid and turned it toward another woman whom he had not seen, the woman waiting with her ill-fed children on that empty range beyond the Little Willow. No one had seemed to think it was worthwhile to carry her the tragic news. No one but himself.

Chapter Three

ANN KINCAID WENT HOME TO HER FATHER'S HOUSE—EIGHT miles as the crow flies, north-by-east of town—and for the last part of the ride she loosed the reins on Stormwind's neck and let the stallion run. She rode like an Indian, her straight young body easy in the saddle, leaning forward to split the pouring wind, her every fiber part of the animal beneath her. With that sailing, incomparable flight she left the two men who were her escort so far behind that they lost sight of her in the long prairies, the willowed dips, the sumac thickets of the rolling land. When Stormwind ran no horse in the country could keep up with him, not even Streaker or any of those others of his clan and kin waiting on the Double K spread.

With a last superb flare and flourish he swept up out of the bottoms, where Bent Bow Creek ran between low banks, and sailed across the flats to stop, with that abrupt and lovely showing of great power perfectly controlled, beside the gate of Big Corral.

Here was the home place of the Kincaid ranch, out from which on the limitless and unfenced range there spread the vast web of Kincaid wealth; namely, the uncounted herds of cattle. Here were buildings of log and stone, barns and sheds and bunkhouse, and the long low house itself.

The peeled white logs had silvered with the years. Sand and stone and the prairie earth itself had taken on the beauty of solid, well-used things. There were hardy vines at the windows and along the wide, dirt-floored veranda with its tree-trunk columns, and a few brave flowers grew in sheltered places safe from the trampling boots of men.

And there were men at the Double K. Men who belonged there, and men who drifted in across the open land, and always it was busy with downright life—the ring of anvil at the blacksmith shop where shoe was set to hoof, the rattle of gear where riders flung saddles on the sapling fences, the jingle of the ever-present spurs. There was talk too, always, usually quiet talk of roundup, beef drive, prices, and the news of all south Texas brought up with the trail herds to Abilene. News of long months with the bawling cattle; of skirmishes with raiders, with Indians, and some-times with disease which decimated the herds and broke their owners. There were Indians here, too. Silent men who made good cow hands, and women who cooked huge quantities of food. And there was Little Fawn who weighed two hundred pounds and whose sway was undisputed in the whole of the female domain.

Ann Kincaid slid off the stallion, left him to Buck No Shirt who reached a brown hand for his rein, and went up the flat stone path toward the house where the big door stood open comfortably across the veranda.

And here, with the first step across the sill, she found sanctuary in the cool and quiet depths of the deep and dusky room. Here there were shadows on the brightest day. Here there were carpets brought by rail and freight wagon half across a continent. Here there was Indian hand-work of basket and gay blanket cheek by jowl with oil paint-ings in their wide gold frames; and here things of the spirit rubbed shoulders with more humble things of bodily com-fort, such as the piano across a far corner and the big arm-chair beside it of hand-hewn, unpainted wood.

Big Red was here in the poor simplicity. The girl was here in the elegance. And all of it came from the man himself, for it was he who had struck the wilderness with an iron hand and made it pour forth riches. A stream, a tide whose largess was to one end only—the setting, the background for his only child, to make of her a lady. How well he had succeeded was evidenced by the fact that, in the twentieth year of her life, she was set apart in a land preponderantly male as something too fine, too high, too beautiful and smart to be of ordinary clay.

And that was Big Red's dream complete.

Now this girl crossed the cool big room and entered another which was her own special and private place. It, too, was richly furnished with four-poster bed and varnished highboy and a priceless full-length mirror against the plastered logs that formed the wall.

She closed the door behind her, tore off her habit with trembling hands, and flung herself down on the bed. She buried her face in the pillow and gave herself up to the flood of tears which she had held in stern abeyance.

She wept with long, hard sobs, but so soundlessly that the hummingbird at the balsam flowers by the window was not disturbed. She cried with a sorrow too old for her bright youth, and it had to do with both things which had been lost that day in front of the Lone Star Palace—the life of a broken man and the integrity of another. For Ann Kincaid did not believe her father's justification of his act.

To her, who loved him above all things in Heaven and earth, Big Red had committed murder.

The sun was gone and long blue shadows darkened down upon the Double K, when finally the door to Ann's room opened softly and without a by-your-leave the mountainous, soft-moving form of the Indian woman was there beside her. She bent down, took the girl under the arms, and turned her over. The black eyes looked deep in the swollen blue ones and Little Fawn grunted, nodded her smooth black head.

Then she sat down and gathered the slim form against her capacious bosom, where she had cradled it against all the ills of childhood.

"Don' know what you cry about," Little Fawn said comfortably, "but you stop now. Ain' nothin' worth it. Ever'-

thing go by, is forget. Man, he take new woman. You cry. 'Nother man. You forget. Baby, it die. You no want live no more. 'Nother baby. You forget. Come on. Most suppertime. Get face washed. Put on clean dress. I hang up you two new ones, all wash, smooth iron. Come now."

She lifted her own weight and that of the girl in an effortless motion, stood the other on her feet, brushed the damp hair back from her forehead, and went out of the room.

Obediently Ann Kincaid did as she had been bidden, and half an hour later sat at the piano in the big room, her hands moving surely over the yellowed keys even though there was no light left of the day nor any lamps lighted. She loved this time, this early darkness, with its mysterious and moving sense of coming things, as if the lone world readied itself for the future with unknown joys, unknown romance. But this night held something sinister and sad because she had seen a flaw in what had been heretofore the perfect stature of a man. Big Red, her idol, had rocked upon his pedestal and the sight had shaken her universe.

So now the nameless and wordless melodies which whispered from her hands were not the bright strains she usually played but of a new and darker pattern. Three riders, squatting on their heels outside in the shadows and listening, after the fashion of every man on the brand when Copper Ann played, let their smokes go out and frowned in wonderment.

Other things were happening in the spring night, too.

In that hidden cabin on the creek in town, Stella Adams waited with calm patience. She sat outside her door, on earth hard-beaten by the feet of men, and waited for that one man of all men in a checkered life whose coming meant the world and all it held. Meant, too, so sick and terrible a nostalgia for an honest life that sometimes she would have wept, if a woman like herself could weep, whose eyes were

dry of that great consolation. She would have given all the
gold money in the tin box on her kitchen shelf, a quite considerable sum, for the homely joys of a modest house, a
backyard where her washing flapped on Mondays and her
neighbor leaned across the fence to gossip of the isolated
world of the little frontier town. And for a man—one man
—to come honestly stamping in the front door to his noon-
day meal.

That man was coming now, his boots heavy on the
planks of the little bridge, erratic with drink and arrogant
with power, and the woman rose to meet him, the heart
shaking in her like that of a young and innocent girl. They
did not speak, but she took his great hand in both of hers
and together they entered the small, dark house. It was
theirs completely, for when Kincaid was in town no other
step ever sounded on the bridge, and here Big Red was king
in a humble kingdom more surely than in that vast domain
eight miles away which he ruled like any monarch.

Here there was no slightest chance of deposition, ever,
eternally.

There the future was unseeable, as all futures in the cattle
country were, dependent on the strength of mind and body
and spirit, of those who had, to hold what they had.

And far out along the Little Willow Creek the rider on
the chestnut horse came finally to a lonely log house, a
cluster of poor buildings set in their small corrals, where a
dim light burned and the open door was outlined in the
starlight. Here a woman waited, too, and she also listened.
She heard what she listened for but it was strange, not the
familiar trot of old Paint, the pinto which Bill Smith had
ridden away that morning toward the town, but the swift
clip-clop of a fresh and heavy horse which took the miles in
stride as if it loved them. This woman, too, rose up beside a
humble door and her heart, too, beat hard against her thin

chest, but for a different reason. Here was fear, the ever-present fear of the underdog watching for what it does not know, ready to take flight or to placate or to plead. She was Elvira Smith, and she had been hungry for a long time, because with the vanishing of their little herd had gone their credit in the town also. The two young children asleep inside the house were hungry, too. She could hear them whimpering uneasily sometimes, beset perhaps by dreams of buttered bread and fried salt meat.

Now she held her breath and stood still as some forest thing beside the door, straining to see who it was riding in toward her from the open plain. When the man and the horse finally came up into the beam of light from the doorway she seemed to let down a little from that taut stance of fear which had held her. This was a stranger, not a rider of those who might wish for more destruction upon her and hers.

She leaned forward, peering, and the man saw the pallor of her face.

"Good evening, Mrs. Smith," he said, in a voice no one had heard for several years. It was soft and slurring just a little, as if its owner might have brushed the edges of the South, that South of fragrance and moonlight on magnolia trees and gardens with ironwork gates; a voice no longer used in daily contact with his fellows. It struck so gently on Elvira's ears that she lost a little more of that nameless fear.

"Good evening," she said.

The man did not dismount, but sat with his hat in his hand, looking down upon her, and she saw that he was handsome in a dark, grave fashion.

His eyes were black as the hair above them and somehow they wore so sorry a look that a new fear crept upon her. It was as if they tried to tell her silently what his lips must tell her shortly.

"You—you—what is it, Mister?" she faltered thinly.

Seeing that she understood, the man stepped out of his saddle and came and stood before her in the light. He had not wanted to startle her by doing so at once.

"Lady," he said, in that velvet voice, "how brave are you? How much can you take and still stand on your two feet?"

"Plenty," she said, grimly. "I've already taken plenty. You—something's happened. To Bill——"

"Yes," the other said. "There was a—a little trouble in the town. Some gunfire."

Elvira Smith was not too strong, and she seemed to sag against the logs behind her. The man put out a hand and steadied her.

"He——" she whispered. "Shot?"

He nodded, still with that firm grasp on her trembling arm.

"Bad? Hurt?"

"Yes, Mrs. Smith."

"Is he—is he——"

"Yes."

At that final and chilling word she crumpled down along the wall and would have fallen, but that the man put both arms around her and held her up.

He held her hard against his breast and smoothed her unkempt hair and let her cry as only the bereft cry in the first black hour of bereavement. He did not speak nor try to stop her, and the weak torrent of her tears stained the fine white shirt, the lapel of the handsome coat, for he had worn his best on this poor errand.

One of the children woke and cried and came stumbling out in its little cotton shift to fling itself against the woman's gaunt legs.

The man reached down and lifted it against its mother's shoulder, so that it put its arms around her neck. At its touch she cried harder and words came mingled with her tears.

"Bill! Oh, Bill!" she sobbed. "Poor Bill! Poor man! He

bore so much, and he was good—so good! But he was half
crazy now, daft and wild and furious."

With the rush of speech the flood of weeping lessened
and she drew herself erect, still in the circle of this strange
man's arm, and began to pour out such a tale of wrong and
poverty and work and sorrow that the hardest heart must
have been touched.

"Work!" she cried bitterly. "Yes, for seven years we
worked like nothing human! Saved and built our little
herd. Went without clothes, sometimes almost without
food! And we were getting ahead! Yes, we were! Our stock
had prospered and we were so proud. Maybe too proud.
Seems like, sometimes, folks get ahead of themselves and
something always happens."

She pushed up her sweated hair.

"It happened to us. To Bill and me and even the children, for they haven't had enough to eat since God knows
when!"

She whimpered again, and the child wailed with her.

The man said gently, "What happened, Mrs. Smith?"

"Something we ain't even dared to mention. We got
cleaned, that's what happened. Every last head, every last
cent we could hope for."

"How? Who?"

Her face, thin and drawn now with her anguish, was
paper-white in the dim light from the kerosene lamp on
the table inside the house, and there was on it the final
courage of utter defeat. Now that there was nothing more
to lose, nothing to fear since the ultimate had happened,
she dared to speak what she and Bill had never put into
words that might be heard by others.

"How?" she said dully. "By the fall beef drive. The great
herds coming down across our spread from roundup, that's
how. Pouring into and through our cattle. And when they
had passed, the prairie where our herd had been was bare
as your hand. Not one head or hide left! Not a yearling or

a calf! Seven years of our lives, Bill's and mine, gone in
thirty minutes! Bill was like a madman that day. I can see
him yet. Riding our old pinto right into the drive, tryin'
to get some of our stock out, waving his arms, screaming
for help. And what did he get?" she finished bitterly.

"What?" the stranger asked.

"They laughed in his face, them riders. They laughed
and yelled and drove faster. When it was over, Bill sat
down right here on this doorstep and cried like a ten-year-
old. He ain't never been the same man since. Fey, sort of,
smouldering and wild inside, though he's been good to us,
kind as a man could be. A man who didn't have anything
to give his family but love. But he gave us that."

There was a dreary pride in the pitiful words, and the
man felt his own anger heighten. "It's an old story," he
said. "I've seen it happen before. In Texas. Now tell me
the rest, Mrs. Smith. Don't be afraid. Nothing more is
going to happen to you and the children. Who did this
thing? Whose cattle were in that beef drive?"

The bottled-up venom of wrong and helplessness spat
in her voice now. "Who?" she said. "Who you s'pose? Who
in this country can do anything he pleases and no questions asked? Kincaid, of course! Big Red Kincaid. The
Double K brand. That's who."

She stopped and drew away, as if the old fear were back
upon her, frightened now that she had poured out the
secret danger to this man whom she had never seen before.

He let her go, and for a long moment he stood looking
beyond her thin shoulder into the starlit night with eyes
that did not see the present but rather a distant past.

"Tell me," the woman said, in a scared tone. "Who
killed my husband?"

The words recalled him to the moment and he met her
question squarely. "You have a right to know," he said. "It
was Kincaid himself. Bill had his rifle, and he tried to kill
the Kincaid horses—it seems they are the top pride of the

Kincaid outfit—and Big Red shot him. You can comfort yourself, Mrs. Smith, that it was instant. He never knew what struck him."

"But I'll know," she said, on a strange note. "I'll always know. And maybe someday the killer himself will know."

"Listen to me, lady," the other said gently. "Forget that thought. You've had enough trouble. And you've got two children, haven't you?"

"Yes," she said, "I have."

"Then you'll have to think of them from now out. You'll have to be their father and their mother both. You'll have no time for revenge. Now, come. You go in and get yourself and them ready to go back to town with me. Have you a team and wagon?"

"Yes. They're out back in the corral."

"Good. I'll hitch them up."

As she turned to obey, Elvira Smith looked back at this strange visitor with questioning eyes. "How come, Mister," she said, "that you're doing this for us? What call you got to bring me word, to help us go see—see"—she swallowed back her tears—"Bill?"

"No call on earth," he said frankly, "except from one human to another. I hate injustice—wrong—whatever you may call such things as this. And a decent man could do no less, once he knew of it."

"I see," she said quietly.

Early morning lay over the town, quiet now after its roaring night. Long rays of sun were almost level along the trampled street where the dust lay in little ridges darkened along their crests by the heavy dew of the plains country. The willows all along the little stream stood tall and lacy against the pale blue sky, stirred by no wind as yet.

Here and there an early rising housewife swept her porch. Jonas Biffle stood on the hotel steps looking up and down the cool, empty road. Jonas ran the Blue Top for Red

Kincaid and tried to juggle profits to his own advantage, secretly. The blacksmith shop was already open. At the hitch rail in front of the Lone Star Palace the plainsman, Sam Bolin, much farther along on his weekly celebration, hung draped over the damp sapling and regarded pensively the dark mess in the dust which no one had taken the trouble to cover.

"'S a shame," he said thickly to the solitude. "Pore feller. He jest went sorta wild, I guess, an' Big Red orten't to a-done it. Ain't no hoss livin' wuth a man's life." He shook his head where the long brown hair hung to his shoulders. Sam was inordinately proud of his hair, and it was the only thing about him which showed care. The rest was frankly casual, to say the least. Now he picked absent-mindedly at his six remaining teeth and hiccoughed sadly. The sorrows of the world pressed down on Sam at times. Times like this, when he had come in from mysterious distances and occupations to spend his few coins on such fleshpots as the town could offer.

Now, as he observed the all but deserted metropolis, things began to happen with that strange nicety of coincidence which so often obtains in the affairs of men. From where the open road came in from the northwest to swing around the town's far end, there were audible the trot and rattle of a team and wagon, the staccato hoofbeats of a saddle horse. And from the willows where the small creek ran a man's boot heels struck hollowly on the plank bridge.

At almost the same moment the shabby outfit with the white-faced woman on the seat and the great red-bearded man came into the open space between the buildings.

Quick, alert, the drink entirely washed out of him by sleep, handsome in his good rider's clothes, Big Red Kincaid took in the situation with one flash of his wild blue eyes. The woman saw him at the same time and half rose to her feet, her hands pulling instinctively on the lines.

Fear flowed over her and then receded as she realized that the time for that was past. She had nothing more to lose that a man might take, and the righteous anger of the wronged rose in her like a tide. She looked at Red Kincaid with hollow eyes and her pale lips opened.

"So!" she said clearly in the morning stillness. "The murderer walks free! High, wide, and handsome! Fine work you've done, Red Kincaid. You stole our cattle and sold them with your drive. Maybe bought that tomboy girl of yours silk clothes, or other pretties she might like, while we went hungry. We're hungry now. Look at these children. Look!" She leaned over and pushed the shrinking little boy upright on the seat. He was thin to emaciation.

"He hasn't had enough to eat for months, since our credit went with our herd. And now you've killed his father. I hope to God you never know a good night's rest from here on out! And that brash girl of yours——"

"Shut up!"

The words spat into the air like the crack of gunfire. Big Red's face flamed from brow to beard with the hot rage that could flare in him so quickly.

"If you say another word——"

He did not finish, for another voice cut in across the carrying quiet of the early day.

"Just a minute," the man on the chestnut horse said sharply. "Kincaid, you're speaking to a lady. Mind what you say."

Big Red whirled on him, too astonished to speak. No one in the whole of the cow country addressed cattle king Kincaid like that. No one dared. He swallowed once and licked the thick lips fallen open in amazement.

"Why, you—you—" he said thickly, "you damned fly-by-night! Get out of my sight!"

"Hardly," the other said. "This woman and her children are here to see their husband and father laid away decently.

And I aim to see that they do so, Kincaid or no Kincaid."

Big Red was feline quick but the stranger struck like an adder.

The gun on Kincaid's thigh was half out of its holster when the other had him covered, and the blunt-barreled weapon had come not from hip or thigh but from beneath its owner's left armpit under the fine black coat. The man on the road's edge was too thunderstruck to move. He stood as he was for a long moment, his hand still on his gun butt and his blue eyes mad with fury.

As if by some magic there were people all up and down the walks by now, witnesses brought by the lifted voices, from saloon and store and the alleyways between them where this and that roisterer had slept off the late hours of play and drink. They stood in silence, though from inside the Lone Star six of the Kincaid riders drew together in a close group by the hitch rail, ready for anything they might be called upon to do.

They were not unnoticed by the man on the big horse. His black eyes missed nothing in the whole dramatic and surcharged scene. And they flicked over something no other saw in that moment; namely, the big stallion halted a little way beyond and the red-haired girl in his saddle. Ann Kincaid, her face pale in the early sun behind her, her soft mouth open. Copper Ann Kincaid, feeling her world rock under her.

Then she saw the most painful thing she had ever beheld. She saw her father, who had never given ground in his life to anyone or anything, whose acts were always right, whose word was never questioned, move slowly on his booted feet and lift his right hand from his thigh.

"And now," she heard that other say, "You get out of our way. If there's anyone in this town who's got the courage to stand on his own feet, will he come forward and help with this matter? Will someone take this woman and her children into the hotel and see that they are fed—I'll pay for it—while I do what's needful at the barber shop?"

For a long moment there was dead silence all up and down the street. No one moved. No one answered.

Then Jonas Biffle, small-souled and dishonest, taking his job and a chance of more than that in his hands, stepped off the hotel steps. He came across the dust, stopped beside the rickety wagon, and held up his hand.

"Morning, Mrs. Smith," he said embarrassedly. "Will you light down?"

Elvira Smith looked once at the man on the chestnut horse and went down over the wheel, stood while Biffle lifted down the boy and girl, and followed him indoors.

With wordless fury in his face, Big Red Kincaid turned and walked away. He joined his men by the hitch rail, took Streaker's rein, mounted, and rode off. His hat was down across his eyes and so it was that he did not see his daughter until he was abreast of her where Stormwind stood against the willows. When he did, the first fruits of that sinister hope which Elvira Smith had voiced fell on him like a blow. He knew in a flash that she had seen and heard. He saw the paleness of her cheeks, the unbelieving sorrow in her eyes.

They did not speak, but the girl turned Stormwind in beside him, her young back straight and stubborn; and riding close together, Big Red and Copper Ann went out of town. One by one their riders followed until there was no sign of the Double K left anywhere in the place. There was only that still form waiting, cleaned and neat, in the barber shop, for that last poor ceremony which would write finis to a life of work and failure; those equally tragic ones he'd left behind him.

And out on the open plain where the peace of a virgin world lay blue and gold about them, the girl leaned over and laid a hand on Big Red's arm.

"Red," she said firmly, "no matter what has happened, no matter what you've done or had to do or may do in the future, to me you're always right, will always be right. I want you to remember that."

What the words cost her in the new uncertainty of her universe only she would ever know. She knew they were a lie, but a lie she had to utter, a bulwark of defense before herself and him, something she must hold to blindly come what may. Only so would her world hold together.

She knew it was a different world, one in which had suddenly appeared distrust where had been perfect trust, a sense of shame and sorrow where had been only pride, and that supremely justified.

She knew she would never forget the scene she had just witnessed, the look of Elvira Smith's white face, her tragic eyes, the sound of her voice in malediction. And she would not forget the thin body of that little boy. The specter of that vanished herd would be with her always.

Something else was destined to be with her also, but of that she had no knowledge yet.

Chapter Four

IN THE WEEK THAT FOLLOWED THESE EVENTS, AN UNACCUS-
tomed quiet lay over the town. Bill Smith had been laid
away in the little cemetery beyond the willowed stream,
and Elvira and her children were gone. They had ridden
out to railhead with Ben Alverson's freight wagons, bound
for that East from which they had hailed in the first place,
she and Bill, with such high hopes of land and stock and
a sure place in the world. And in the woman's shabby bag
was more money than she had seen in all the years of her
tenure here. It had been given her by the black-clad stranger
in exchange for her homestead right, the log house, the
ancient wagon and team, the pinto saddle horse. When
she had protested honestly it was too much he had patted
her work-hard hand and smiled with grim satisfaction.

"Never you mind, Mrs. Smith," he had said. "There's
something of poetic justice in this money. I won it in a
poker game at Kincaid's place, so you have a double right
to it. It will see you safely back among your people and, if
you use it carefully, should provide for you and the children
for a long time. Your Bill would be happy to know that."

Elvira's eyes filled up with tears in which gratitude was
mixed with sorrow. "Yes," she said, "he would. And I'll
keep it and use it to the best possible purpose. And I'll
never forget you, Mister, as long as I live, for the best man
I have ever known."

And she bent suddenly and brushed her pale lips against
the sleeve of the fine black coat. It was the purest accolade
of honor a man could ever have, and the gambler flushed
painfully beneath his dark skin.

So the killing of a nondescript man, the travail of his

colorless wife, the wrong done his helpless children were things of the past in a matter of days, forgotten or glossed over after the loose manner of the time and place.

But the country had a new landowner, the town a new citizen, for the stranger in the fine clothes had suddenly become a part of both. He hired Sam Bolin to live in the Smith cabin and look after the three horses, the cow and calf, the few scrawny chickens, and the shepherd dog—and the town awoke one morning in the second week to blink and rub its eyes and blink again at the brand-new sign above the door of Dick Burley's saloon and gambling hall, the Silver Tip, which carried the words in bold black letters, JOHN VELANTRY, PROP.

So the mysterious stranger had a name at last, a setting and a background. He had paid Dick Burley in cash, so there had been more than clothing in the roll behind the low-built saddle, and the town was pricked with sharp and sudden interest in this rider out of nowhere who could so boldly champion the underdog and who had dared to throw a gun on Big Red Kincaid himself. Talk was rife. The town buzzed with it. A guarded excitement underlay the speculations as to what would happen next, what Big Red would do about it.

Dick Burley took his sudden wealth and drifted off with the first freight teams east, and John Velantry was suddenly a fixed and vital part of the community. He settled in at the Silver Tip, overhauled its entire setup, tore out the hidden "fix" beneath the roulette wheel, fired the faro dealer, rehired the bartender, and laid down a set of rules which soon became known for the fairest in any gambling house west of Abilene. And he himself became more elegant, more brushed and burnished, the white shirts beneath the black silk ties more meticulously spotless. He moved himself from the Blue Top Hotel, finding that it was short of rooms; the chestnut horse from its stable for a like reason. He fixed up living space in the back of the saloon, had a small lean-to built close to its back door for the chestnut, and was as solidly entrenched as though he'd been there always.

For himself he seemed to have rules also, plainly laid down and rigidly adhered to, which included long hours in the saddle daily. These rides, always in the early morning, took him out across the levels where tall white yuccas bloomed and the small blue and white daisies nodded in the little winds. This was the country of the Great Grass Plains, lush with verdure, beautiful to look upon, pitted with forsaken buffalo wallows, for already the great black herds had been decimated by the ruthless hunters of the "dollar a hide" era, stretching away into infinity south toward the Border, west toward the vast and gently rising ramp of the Continental Divide. Spread upon it now were other herds, the motley colored, half wild hordes of the longhorns. Tall, rangy, their monstrous horns slightly curved and uniformly horizontal at right angles from their heads, reaching a spread of from six to eight feet from tip to tip, they covered the earth like a blanket. And as far as the eye could see they belonged to the Double K brand. To Big Red Kincaid and so, potentially, to Copper Ann. They looked like a monarch's heritage, and so they were, in a land where human needs could not be otherwise than simple, though it had not been so long since the price of a steer had been half a dollar; the cost of its branding the same.

But now, with Abilene and railhead forming an avid market for the states east of the Mississippi, they were another matter.

Big Red Kincaid was rich. He had prospered mightily and fast.

How much of that prospering had been honest and natural no one could say. How much had come by way of those vast beef drives that rolled across the plains and over everything in their way no one even ventured a guess. No one, that was, excepting poor Elvira Smith, who had no more herds to lose.

Long thoughts like these passed through the alert mind of the rider on the chestnut horse day after day as he took those seemingly aimless journeys, skirting the edge of the open, keeping along the willowed streams, sitting for long spaces of time in this mesquite thicket or that, counting a thousand head of cattle, measuring after a fashion the amount of land they covered. It was a slow and inaccurate method of gauging a man's wealth, but it was method of a sort. And this man desired to know all he could find out about the man who had become his enemy. For that Kincaid was, and would always be, his enemy he had no slightest doubt. An enemy of parts, with potentialities and powers and the ruthlessness to use them. To any other man in the country that situation would have been a source of grave concern. John Velantry did not underestimate its danger nor deny its concern. He did not admit its fear.

And slowly, bit by bit, he learned more about Big Red Kincaid. From the talk of men who gambled at the Silver Tip. From their attitude, from their silences when Big Red was mentioned, and from the fact that most of them who ran cattle on this northern edge of the Llano Estacado did so to the south and west of town, away from that limitless northeastern world which was, as by a common consent, the Kincaid stamping ground. For three long years John Velantry had lived on the constantly westward-pushing fringes of the cattle herds. For three years he had drifted here and there, always a man of mystery, living by the cards, stopping a month here, another there, and always studying some tycoon of the trail, the drive, the bulging moneybags of prosperity. And always failing to find what he looked for, always moving on. Always alone and womanless. And always with that bit of cold chilled steel where his heart should have been.

But here, at last, he had struck root. Here he felt a wind

of premonition blowing gently through the soft spring days. Here there was a tightening within him, a tautening of the strings of his spirit, a brightening of old memories usually pushed down and under the sullen tide of an iron-hard resolution, because they were too painful to be lived with on the surface. And this feeling had come alive in him with the small and sordid tragedy of Bill Smith and Elvira. Between that and another far back in his youth a tie had lifted, strong and compelling, like a cable out of dust. A thing of verisimilitude and ruthlessness, of likeness and coincidence too strong to be passed over.

So once again Velantry had stopped in his wanderings to study a man, his past and his present. And this time he felt that he would stay. For now again he had come upon a man of wealth and power, of arrogance and pride and ruthlessness. A big man with red hair. A man whose ways and habits seemed to check with old word pictures in his mind, whose age seemed approximately right. A type of man whom Velantry had hunted through the frontier for three years.

So he settled down to the running of his new emprise, the Silver Tip, and was more content than he had been for many moons. Always contained, he became still more reserved. Courteous of manner in a time and place where manners had loosened with a looser way of life, he stood somewhat alone among the populace. And it was inevitable that these things should throw about him a mantle of romance among the women of the town.

"Mr. Velantry," they said among themselves, guardedly, "he's different. He lifts his hat to old Aunt Hannah Ames just like he does to any of us younger ones."

"Yes, but," someone said a trifle ruefully, "he bows to Stella Adams when she walks in the evenings just the same, too. Do you suppose——?"

"My man says no," another took it up. "They say around the saloons that he's a lone wolf. Say he never talks of women at all. Only smiles at the jokes, never makes them himself."

"Maybe he don't like women. There are men like that. Disappointed in love, maybe, sometime, and forsworn the whole tribe."

"No, I don't think so. He gave the Kincaid girl her gloves to grip that day in the street. From what the men say, she needed something to hold to then. They say she sort of weaved on her feet when she looked on what her father'd done, that her eyes were sick and terrible. She may be a hoyden, but Big Red is her sun, moon, and stars. Him and that ramping stud she rides. She was like a person struck with a mortal wound, the menfolks say, and no one but the stranger saw and understood. And there was Elvira Smith. No, he don't hate women, and he's not indifferent. He just don't seem to think about them."

"Well, he won't dare do any thinking about Stella Adams anyway, or Big Red will kill him."

But the other shook her head. "No," she said with a far insight, "Kincaid will kill no man over Stella Adams, for his girl would hear of it. Over men's doings, yes, but not over the town's woman. He'd quicker kill the man that told Copper Ann about him and Stella—and every man jack in the country knows it. For if the girl loves Big Red above all things, she is his god. The men say so and they should know, who know them both so well, for the gaming tables know Copper Ann as well as any man who frequents them."

"The hussy!"

"No," the other speaker said, "she is no hussy. The men say she's clean as a hound's tooth, a straightshooter, upright and good. If they weren't safely married, half the men in this town would be in love with her. Maybe they are anyway. She's beautiful enough to turn the head of the soberest."

And as the women made their appraisal of the stranger in their midst, so had the men, long back. Two weeks back, to be exact, when John Velantry came riding into town that early morning beside the wagon of Elvira Smith. Made it with his first sharp words to Red Kincaid, his open championing of the family the other had despoiled, his utter disregard for the cattle king and all he meant.

"He's got guts," they said later. "No man was ever closer to his death than when Big Red reached for his gun. And he never batted an eye."

"Looks like he's square, too," someone opined. "He fired Sim Butts because he found out his finger ends was sanded. Sim was a fancy dealer, right profitable to Dick Burley."

But among all this talk one man was silent—Ben Alverson, who ran the biggest string of freight teams west of Abilene.

"What you think of Velantry, Ben?" someone asked the freighter.

"I got nothing to say," the big man answered. "I don't know anything about him."

Speculative eyes regarded Alverson in silence, and then another shrugged the matter off.

"May be all right, but I never did like a long-tailed coat."

"Coat don't make a man, Tom," the barber said. "He took it off and washed Bill Smith himself, so he'd look well as possible to his wife."

And so the matter of John Velantry stood among them.

Chapter Five

ANN KINCAID CAME OUT OF THE DEEP ROOM AND CROSSED THE hard dirt floor of the veranda. The earth, wet down by Little Fawn's daily sprinkling, the heavy boots of men pounding upon it always, was hard as concrete, smooth and level. There were hand-hewn chairs set here and there, worn to a satiny shine, and a keg-stave hammock swung across one end. Here the master of the Double K sat often in the heavy heat of afternoon, the cool of evening, to smoke his pipe and gaze upon his domain. From here the wide level spread away, dropping a little, to where the slow creek moved among its trees; the long low barns, the many corrals, lay to the left, with beyond them the only bit of fencing on the place. This was the big pasture, bisected by cross fences, where the prides of the Double K, the horses of the Fingermarks, lived and moved and had their being.

And of all the beauty that lay so lavishly on the virgin world about, they were the peak and pinnacle, the end and aim and crowning glory, as it were. They were the only ones of their kind, so far as anyone knew, west of the Mississippi, and they numbered only ten in all.

They were a mysterious and unexplainable breed, destined to early extinction; for of them all, only one was able to perpetuate them, old Thunderfoot, the matriarch, and she was now sixteen years old. In her lifetime she had dropped nine foals, three colts and six fillies, but every mare was barren, no stud had ever reproduced his kind. There were Bluefire and Sunbolt and Stormwind, the stallions; Streaker and Cyclone, Flyer and Skimmer, Breezy and Hotwind, the mares. And they were the fastest runners

46

in the country. No one accurately knew their speed, for there was nothing on the plains to judge them by. They ran like the living things that lay behind their names, flame and wind and storm, and to ride them was an experience of a lifetime, though there were few who had experienced it. For Red Kincaid was jealous of them as any lover of his mistress.

And only Big Red knew their origin, or such of it as was knowable. This dated back to sixteen years ago, when Big Red was a younger man, only four years on the Double K, with a wife, and one small girl child, and a towering ambition to make himself the richest, most powerful man north of the Llano Estacado. He rode his own domain those days, long drifting journeys over virgin grasslands where wild cattle grazed among the thinning buffalo herds, and thought long thoughts of wealth and high station among men. And here, on a warm spring day, he threaded down among the sumac thickets of a flat beside a little stream, to come suddenly upon something that lay like a small blue jewel where the sunlight dappled down among the leaves. It lay flat upon the bedded earth, its tiny ribs staring with starvation, and it was a week-old blue roan filly. Not white or black with the baby coat that would shed off later to show its adult, basic color, but blue at birth; and that was a phenomenon.

For a long moment Red Kincaid sat looking down upon this dead thing in the thicket, wondering why its mother had abandoned it to starve slowly, what had happened to her. Wolves, maybe, or a rattler hidden by some rock.

And then he bent forward in his saddle, his sharp eyes narrowed, for he had seen, or thought he'd seen, the barest movement beneath the silken hide. He thought the baby breathed. And so it had, the sighing, long-spaced breath of the dying or near dead, and in a second the man was off his horse and on his knees beside it, his huge hand laid gently over the tiny heart. At his touch the small face, white-blazed under the fuzzy blue foretop, lifted weakly, one pencil-like foreleg struggled out.

It was then that Red Kincaid laid eyes for the first time on the strange mark that was to distinguish this infinitesimal creature and others after it from all the world of its species. For on the inside of the little knee, splashed across the lighter blue, were four sharp straps of brilliant black, as if a tarry hand had slapped it.

"Fingermarks!" Big Red had said aloud, wonderingly. "Just like the marks of four fingers!"

And so he gave the breed a name. For he took the starveling home across his saddle bow and coddled it back to life with cow's milk and the tender care of Jenny, his wife, and it lived and thrived.

It was Jenny who, when the filly was six months old, had given it a name. Watching the young thing race against the wind one day in fall, its soft mane like a smoke above its outstretched neck, its small bright hoofs making music on the sod, she had laughed and clapped her hands.

"Thunder! Hear it, Red!" she'd cried, laughter on her lighted face. "The long roll of a storm! Thunderfoot! Thunderfoot the Runner!"

So Thunderfoot the blue roan was from that day on, with something of the elements in every name of all her get beyond her—and something of Jenny in them, too. Jenny, who did not live out that winter.

So Big Red was left alone in the wilderness he had chosen, with his lost and lonely child, his growing herds, his gathering nucleus of riders to handle them, his gradually widening range, his house and its possessions, his ambitions, and his sparse and priceless treasures, the horses of the Fingermark. That small, strange group, unable to reproduce itself, given to him by the one mare, Thunderfoot, dowered with her beauty and her miraculous speed, forever set aside by the sign-manual of their natural and unduplicable brand. A wild, heady, masterless breed, erratic and spirited, and always of two colors, no matter to what stud their dam was bred. Red roan, blue roan; the former with manes and tails of pinkish ivory, those of the latter a clear and shining silver. The linings of the red roans' ears, the edges of their nostrils, the stockings on their slender legs were a rich dark bay; those of the blue roans black.

And every face, beneath its pink or silver foretop, was white.

A slim, clean blaze running from forehead to muzzle intensified the large, excitable eyes, brought out their shining grace.

These were the Fingermarks, these ten racing things of hot blood and incomparable beauty, and their fame went down the Chisholm Trail to Texas, west to the Rockies, wherever plainsmen, scouts, and riflemen foregathered.

Men hearing of them came long distances to see them. Many tried to buy them, and there had been attempts to steal them outright. But no man's money was adequate, no thief could break the cordon of watchfulness around them.

And next to his daughter Big Red loved them, if an inordinate pride in them could pass as such. Ann loved them, too, but in a different manner. With pride, yes, but with a passion of tenderness that brought a mist of tears to her eyes, a trembling of excitement in every fiber of her body, when she saw them run.

Now as she reached the pasture gate, a smile of pure, joyous affection was on her face, which had been so grave since the events of the past fortnight. Spread out on the green levels the roans looked like big flowers in a giant's garden, or monstrous jewels on a velvet cloth.

She watched them awhile, then put two fingers to her lips and sent a sharp, clear whistle to cut the quiet air. At the sound the handsome heads came smartly up, and here and there a whistle answered her, but only one did more than that. Stormwind, the pick of the pack, the wildest, fastest, most beautiful of them all, and her own property, shook his great mane and came to her on the run. She reached her hands across the sapling gate and the stallion sniffed them, blowing, expecting the tidbit they always brought. Not finding it, the bit of sugar, the crust of bread, he arched his huge neck, laid back his ears and, breasting up against the gate, nuzzled her shoulder, her arm, with no gentle touch, half knocking her off her feet, so that she had to catch the pole to right herself.

"You old devil!" she said fondly. "You ruffian! Ann's darling! Here." From a pocket in her dress she fished a piece of cornbread and watched him eat it avidly, gave him the palm of her hand to lick for the last crumb. Then she opened the gate and, taking him by the foretop, led him toward the barns and Big Corral. Here she bridled him and flung her sidesaddle across his back, expertly tightened its double cinch. In a matter of moments she was on his back and gone like a bolt, like a wind, out across the long stretch of the flat toward the creek. Always they went so, in full flight from a standing start, and a wild excitement was in them both from that first loin-dropped leap.

Big Red and three of the riders, coming in from the northern range, saw them go, and Kincaid frowned.

"Wish she wasn't so set on going by herself," he grumbled. "Someone ought to follow her. That big blue devil might kill her some day."

"Hell!" Sloan, the foreman, said. "You know better, Red. No Fingermark would—or could—throw Ann. She's the best rider west of Abilene."

"Could hit a prairie dog hole," Red muttered.

"Not with her aboard. She sees everything within a mile. And she hates a bodyguard. You never see the tricks she pulls to lose the boys who trail her when she wants to be alone with Stormy. Dodge into a thicket, hide down the creek, or just plain let him out and run away, clear out of sight."

"I know," Red answered, and rode moodily into the home place. He had been another man since the incident in the street in town when he had made a deadly motion and a younger man had beaten him to it. His roaring laughter had deserted him, and a sullen anger seemed to ride him at all times. The men understood and kept a careful guard on word and look, and the big man brooded. Hatred was growing in him like a weed, a violent and furious hatred of the stranger in the black coat. He felt a desire to crush him so deadly strong it caused a definite sickness in his stomach, shut the thick lips beneath the red beard into a traplike line. Few times in his life had Red Kincaid felt so, but always the feeling had been followed by action so ruthless, so final, that the sickness passed, leaving him his roaring, jovial self again, once more master of his world.

Ann and Stormwind sailed across the flat, hit the ford above the sandy riffle, splashed through the knee-deep water, and came up on the open levels to the south. That way and to the west the town lay, and she had no wish to go there, so she turned due west along the stream and for a long time gave herself up to the high intoxication of racing speed, of sunlight and pouring wind, and the song of thunder that was Stormy's running feet. As violence could calm Big Red, so these things could lift her heart from any sorrow she had known. They lifted her now, set laughter on her face once more. She wore a common dress of bright blue gingham, open at the neck and buttoned down her slim front, and her hair was like a copper crown shining in the sun.

When Stormwind ran he went in so straight a line that there was no rocking sidewise motion, and the girl in the fine saddle sat as easily as in a chair, her right arm swinging with the rhythm of his stride. So they went west along the winding creek beside the willows, and Ann forgot the world and all it held except this drunkenness of speed, the

monstrous engine of power and beauty that was the racing
thing beneath her.

They left the home place far behind and were alone in
the swinging cup of the universe, blue above and green
below, dotted with the grazing herds of the longhorns.
Yet they were not alone, for a rider on a chestnut horse
sat watching them from the shelter of a sumac thicket, and
there was a strange expression on his dark face. A look of
wonder at this speed, of wistful sadness at the unspeakable
beauty of these two wasted on the empty land. As they
neared him, John Velantry touched the chestnut and moved
into the open. His appearance almost in their path was like
an electric shock to horse and rider. Stormwind slowed
so sharply that his front hoofs plowed the earth in two long
furrows, reared and squealed in the instant fury of the
stallion at a strange horse in his domain. His ears were flat
against his head, his mouth half open, his blue eyes flashing
wildly. The girl on his back was no less shocked, no less
instantly angry. This was the man who had shamed Big
Red before his men and all those others in the town, here
on Red's own land! Something of Red's intolerance rose
in her. She looked at him with blazing eyes.

"You!" she exploded. "What are you doing here?"

John Velantry removed his wide black hat, held it against
his knee. The sun on his black hair brought out a shine of
blue like that on a crow's wing.

"Why," he said politely, "I was just looking at the
country."

"Well, this is our country, Big Red's country," she said
insolently, "and you're not welcome in it."

"Perhaps not," he answered, "but not all this land is
patented, you know. Much of it still belongs to the govern-
ment—free range—and any man is free to ride it."

The girl's lips fell apart in wordless astonishment at this
heresy, and the man saw the beauty in their bright curves,
the pearl-white teeth between. Then she shut them to a

tight line much like Big Red's, when his anger was beyond words, and gathered Stormy's reins hard in both hands.

"You'd better not led Red hear that," she said grimly. "And now please move aside."

There was studied insult in the words, for she had all the open plain to ride, and Velantry's face flushed darkly. He did not move.

"I had thought, Miss Kincaid," he said with a faint contempt, "that you were somewhat different. I thought you cared, just a little, that day in town—that there was a certain softness in you. I was mistaken. You are Big Red's daughter indeed, true princess of the Kincaid kingdom. I might have known."

He bowed politely, drew the chestnut back a little that she might pass in her chosen line of progress, and as she urged the stallion forward against his will to stay and fight this dark intruder, she said across her shoulder a thing that fired Velantry's own temper.

"Take that horse away from here. We don't like scrub stock on this range."

Then she was gone once more at a racing run, and the man looked after her with angry eyes.

"You hear that, Ring?" he said softly. "Scrub! You! My Heaven!"

He leaned to the right, shook out his rein, and in another second he too was gone along the levels toward the west. He, too, rode easily as an Indian, and there was no rocking motion in the level running of the big brown horse beneath him. No one in the town had seen the chestnut run. They would have been astonished now. Long, low, level, smooth as water flowing, this stranger come from nowhere began to close the gap between himself and Stormwind. Lighter, more slenderly built, he made less noise upon the grassy earth, and Ann Kincaid, enveloped in the vast thunder of the stallion's flight, did not hear the long roll of his coming.

It was not until a hand touched her arm on the left that she flashed a startled glance that way and saw the man's grim face close to her own.

"Don't call a horse a scrub until you see him run, Princess," he said mockingly. "Next time I'll give you twice as long a start."

Then he reined away and went southwest toward the town at an easy lope, and the girl on the blue horse watched him go, her face as white as milk. It was not the anger now which set that look upon her features. It was the memory of a rider left behind who'd closed the gap, caught up with Stormwind. Stormwind, the fastest-known thing north of the Llano Estacado! It was a trick, she told herself furiously, a low advantage he had taken. If she had known he was behind her she'd have touched the stallion's shoulder and left him like an arrow.

But the glory was gone from the day, and she crossed the creek and returned home at a gentle pace, and the anger at this man was deep and heavy in her. Something else lay deeper still—a sorrow, a sadness, a disillusionment. There had been the first faint rift of failure in her solid world and she was bewildered, peering fearfully through half-opened portals to a future which she could not see, but which held dark shadows of portent, she knew as surely as that she lived.

Big Red and Stormy. In the hitherto untouched perfection of them both there was the dim beginning of a flaw. Red had killed a man without sure justification. The king of all racers had been overtaken in his stride. And the first man in her knowledge of men had spoken to her mockingly, called her Princess in derision, ascribed to her a hardness in the matter of Bill Smith's killing which was far from true.

She still could not bear to think of that, could not forget a woman's tears, the half-starved thinness of a little child, and a tightness took her throat at memory of them now. This man was hard himself to taunt her with that memory.

Hard and cold and somehow dangerous. His black eyes had been just now like deep dark wells in winter. She shivered with a new, strange apprehension. She who had never feared anything or anyone in all her life before.

And so she came to Big Corral in a silence and a gravity which sat oddly on her, gave Stormy over to Buck No Shirt, and went slowly to the house where evening shades were already soft and cool in the big room. There was no one about, and an easy quiet lay over the familiar place. Over at the bunkhouse a couple of the boys were singing some sentimental ditty of range and trail, and Little Fawn came noiselessly to stand in the kitchen door and look at her. Her sloe-black eyes smiled softly, for this was her ewe lamb.

"Where's everyone?" the girl asked. "Where's Red?"

"To town," the woman answered comfortably. "All go but Pete an' Al. Go get drunk, gamble off shirts. Fool men."

Ann sank into the big chair by the piano and lay back, sprawling in a loose, manlike way that always made Big Red furious.

"Stop that!" he would say when he saw her so. "Sit up! Put your feet together! You're a lady and by hell and high water you'll act like one!"

The girl would look up at him with something of his own insolence and laugh in his face. "I don't want to be a lady, Red," she'd say sometimes, "and what if I won't be?"

"Then I'll take the rawhide to you!" he had answered once, and all the laughter had left the girl's eyes.

"You do just once," she'd said softly, "and I'll hate you till I die."

The anger left the man's face as if a hand had wiped it, and so sick a look had come there instead that Ann had jumped to kiss him, to grasp his great beard and shake the leonine head in quick contrition.

"If you ever do that, daughter," Red had said profoundly, "I'll blow my brains out pronto. There'd be no need to live."

And she had known it to be the downright truth.

All that Big Red wanted, was, and did was, in the long run, for her sake, a carpet for her young feet, a background for her life.

And now she lay in the big chair and thought about men, her elbows on the armrests, the tips of her fingers pushing the damp curls back from her temples. Little Fawn was silent, and presently Ann spoke.

"I thought I knew men, Fawn," she said, "but I've found out lately that I don't. There are things in them no woman knows, I think."

"Certain sure," the Indian woman said. "How come you find that out now? You know all men here from way back. You find new man?"

"Yes," Ann answered frankly, "I find new man. New devil. Man who dares—who dares——"

The dark woman smiled in the shadows. "Man dares stan' up 'gainst you? Man laughs, mebbe?"

The girl sat up suddenly. "Yes, damn him!" she said explosively. "Yes, he did! And I hate him, poison hard!"

Little Fawn shook her head, and there was concern in her voice. "That bad," she said, "ver' bad. Make think 'bout that man too much. Better forget, like I say 'fore time. More better all ways."

"You don't forget," Ann said harshly, "an outlander who comes on your own place and calls your hand, tells you what a skunk you are, tries cheap tricks to show you up!"

"H'm," Little Fawn said. "H'm'm'm."

Ann rose without more words. "Guess I'll go to bed," she said. "I'm kind of tired."

"Supper?" the woman said. "Got good stew, fresh bread."

"No supper," the other answered. "Not hungry."

Chapter Six

RED KINCAID, WITH SEVEN MEN BEHIND HIM, CAME INTO town like a whirlwind. Streaker, ramping in corral for all the days when her master sulked, given only small goings among the cattle, was violent and full of fire. Her pink foretop blew back between her red-lined ears; her eyes were flashing stars of beauty in her white-blazed face. Next to Stormwind she was the greatest of the Fingermarks. Now she thundered down the dusty street and slid spectacularly up to stop beside the hitch rail at the Lone Star. Big Red stepped out of saddle, lithe and easy as a youth, knotted her rein, and stamped up the steps. Behind him Sloan and Harris, Fisher, Spink, and Farloe, Bryce, and Starbuck secured their mounts in like fashion, and all but the last two followed the boss into the saloon. These two, after the hard and fast rule of the outfit, lounged by the rail, a guard for these horses which meant so much to the Double K. And a beautiful sight they were in the rose and lavender of the coming twilight—Bluefire, blue as Stormy; Sunbolt red; Hotwind and Cyclone and the Skimmer red; Breezy and Flyer blue under their silver manes. They looked unearthly, like horses of the Camargue, or the mounts of gods racing the skies from Olympus, and always they drew their mead of silent homage from the men of plain and trail and distant mountain slope who stopped in their roistering to look upon them.

They took great windy breaths after their racing run and whistled loudly in the quiet air.

There were strangers in the town this night, brown, hard-bitten men in the worn and sometimes ragged clothes of long riding in the open land; for the first trail-herd of the

spring, harbinger of the driving season, was camped six
miles away on the crossing of Pond Creek's upper fork. It
was a small herd, for it had lost half its number to a raiding
band of Arapaho Indians, more in the quicksands of the
South Canadian. These men who brought the remnant
north were disillusioned, brittle of speech, hair-trigger-hung
for fight or gamble, drink or dissipation. They had drifted
up the Chisholm Trail from middle Texas, bound for Abilene and the profits and pleasures to be found there, only
to find themselves shorn of much of that bright prospect
by the vicissitudes of the times and the undertaking. At
the ford on Upper Pond they had seen the deep plowed
furrow, the piles of sod, leading off to north and west toward the town, after the fashion of the day where settlements sprang up, a frank signpost of such primitive civiliza-
tion as might be found short of their journey's end. So they
had bedded down the weary cattle, left night guard by
drawing lots, and come jogging in along the dusty street
eager for such fleshpots as the tiny place might afford.

There were eleven of them, headed by the owners, Frank
and Seastron Daunce, and they went in a body up the steps
and into the Lone Star Palace. They left their horses, trail-
thin, trail-hard as their masters, tied a little way beyond the
Fingermarks, but every man jack of them stopped to look
at the Kincaid stock. No one spoke a word, but every man
in the group had a quick and guilty thought of the gold
such unbelievably handsome creatures would bring among
the rich, flamboyant tycoons in the flaunting new town at
railhead. Not one among them had ever seen their like.
Because there was not their like among the smaller, com-
moner wild horses of the plains.

But in this trigger-hung frontier no man looked too long
at another man's possessions, either his mount, his cattle,
or his woman, so they took their astonished eyes away and
went on into the saloon. They lined along the bar and
tossed raw liquor down their drink-starved, dusty throats

and could not be satisfied. Most of them proceeded to get happily drunk, but the two bosses, Frank and Seastron Daunce, were not of these. No man with his all at stake and dependent on his own alertness in the time and place could afford to lose his wits.

So the brothers had several moderate potions and turned to the gaming tables. They had some money with them and both were sane and crafty players, and their game was poker. They won a sizable amount in the next two hours, and Big Red Kincaid left his monte table to come and stand a little way apart and watch them. Again, no man watched a player at his game. At least not pointedly. Ordinarily Kincaid would not have done so either. But he was not himself these days. Not since that furious day in the open street when his arrogance had first been broached, and it took little to set the restlessness, the moody and sullen anger that seemed always near the surface, to swift and unpredictable action. Now he stood with his great legs apart, his thumbs in his wide leather belt, and looked down upon the table full of men with his excitable blue eyes. He stood so for so long that Frank Daunce glanced sidewise at him several times, a glance that reached at first no higher than the wrinkled boots, the heavy trousers tucked into their stitched tops, but which presently rose along his middle and stopped upon his bearded face. Daunce laid down his cards, a slow, deliberate motion, turned half round in his chair.

"Well?" he said mildly. "What is it, Mister?"

"Eh?" Kincaid said, startled. "What's what?"

"You seem unduly interested in my hand—hands, I should say. You've studied them enough."

"Studied?" Red said sharply. "Hell! Can't a man look over the games in his own place? You got a chip on your shoulder?"

For a tensing moment the man at the table sat quietly. Then he rose, a tall, lean man of early middle age. His eyes were small and topaz colored and there was a curtain in them behind which few men had ever looked. Farther south and west, deep in the Llano Estacado, he had been known to kill a man for less than this. But now he spoke softly, moved softly, and Seastron Daunce moved, rose as softly, laid down his own cards. It was Frank who talked, usually, and the other who acted.

Now Frank set a wintry smile on his features, moved the chair he had just occupied back to the table. With his trail-herd bedded down six miles away he wanted no trouble here, meant to have none, though a hot resentment was in him.

"I reckon there's other places in this here town where a man can find a game," he said amiably. "Come on, Stron."

He walked swiftly toward the door, calling loudly to his men, who left their places and drew in behind him. They clattered out and down the steps into the street where twilight had thickly fallen and the lights from the saloons, the hotel, made golden beams across the dust. They stood in a bunch and looked for the likeliest place, and Stella Adams, walking in the dusk on the beaten path across the way, turned her handsome face toward them.

These men were a half-lawless type and they had been long months away from womankind, and the sight of her was like a whiplash on raw skin. Two of them stepped out to cross the street but stopped suddenly when a gun cracked smartly from the doorway of the Lone Star Palace behind them. The dust from the bullet rose in a tiny puff not four feet from the woman's swinging skirt and stood for a lazy moment before her like a hooded snake, dire with portent, picked out sharply in the Lone Star's beam of light. She lifted her eyes and looked up at Big Red standing in that lighted door, and something like a flash of secret joy passed over them. She turned her face away and moved sedately on. This was her nightly promenade, out to the end of the scattered buildings and back again to the hidden bridge, across it to the still more hidden cabin. It was her advertisement, the sign-manual of her ancient trade, but this night it would be void of profit save and except that great and wasted treasure of her life, the service of unsanctified love.

She had not known Big Red was in town. He had not been in for many days. Now no other mattered. There was nothing else of import in the universe. How long she might have to wait beside her shadowed doorway would not matter, either, for sooner or later he would be there, if not this night, then the next, his boot heels erratic on the sounding planks of the bridge, his body hot with drink, his wild blue eyes on her face a moment in the candlelight before she blew it out.

In the street the strangers from the Chisholm Trail drew together in tight silence and turned west toward the rest of town. They passed the Blue Top Hotel, the Odeon, and were heading uncertainly past the Silver Tip toward the Double K, when Frank Daunce stopped them with a hand held out.

He leaned forward, pushed up his hat, and peered at the handsome figure coming along the street and about to pass. A tall figure, slim and graceful in its elegant black clothes.

"Well, I'll be damned!" Daunce almost shouted. "Johnny! Johnny Velantry or I'm a liar!"

He strode forward like a panther, caught the other by the shoulders, and swung him toward the light from the Silver Tip the better to scan his face. "Old Johnny in the flesh!"

Velantry caught Frank's hand and pumped it hard, laughing in instant pleasure. "Sure! Sure!" he cried. "Well, you old polecat! Where you been? Where you going? How come?"

He had fallen instantly into the idiom of the trail and cow camp, his speech like Frank's. "What you doing here?"

"Trail-herd," Daunce answered. "Bound for Abilene. Started with a good bunch. Met Arapaho raiders. Lost half. More in quicksand on the South Canadian. Tryin' to get the rest to railhead. Been a hell of a bad trip. Bedded at furrow-end on trail. Come over here for a little fling. Stopped yonder"—he nodded toward the Lone Star—"but some damned redheaded shitepoke's a bit too fresh over there, so we come away. But what you doing here? Ain't seen you since a year, year and a half, at Caddo Springs ——"

"Year and quarter," Velantry interrupted him. "Not Caddo. Rush Springs."

"That's right. On a chestnut horse."

"Still got it. Best horse in a thousand miles."

"Seen them roans tied back yonder?"

"Sure. But Ring is still the best."

"Who them roans belong to?"

"That redhead you just met."

"Be dam'! But how come yourself, Johnny?"

"Settled here."

"Settled? You settled?"

"Yes. I bought this place." He waved toward the Silver Tip.

"I'd never of thought it," Frank Daunce said. "Never knew as travelin' a feller as you in my born days. Seen you an' heard of you from East Texas to th' Capitans, from th' Concho to th' Pecos and back again. Always seemed like you was drove by somethin' inside you."

He stopped in sudden embarrassment, for as he had flared at Kincaid's watching of his game, so Velantry had a right to flare at the mention of something so purely personal as where he went and why.

But Velantry laughed and laid a hand on Frank's faded shirt sleeve, drew him toward the saloon. "Come on in," he said. "There's drink and cards in here just as good as any at the Lone Star. The house is yours tonight. And yours too, Stron," he added, reaching to shake Seastron's hand, overlooked for the moment of the hilarious meeting.

Laughing, eager, with their men trailing behind them, the Daunces followed Johnny Velantry into the Silver Tip. They were tired and dusty, wo n with weeks of work and riding, depressed by the losses f their venture, and Velantry's warm and friendly greeting seemed to put new life in them.

As Frank Daunce had said, the trails of Velantry and these two brothers had crossed in a number of out of the way places, and they knew little about each other. Little that would bear discussion. Velantry, the mysterious rider with the good clothes in his saddle roll, the expert gambler's hands, silent for the most part, minding his own business. The rangy, hard-bitten Daunces, ragged-poor for months on end, then flaunting new affluence, bragging of a cattle drive now and again, though where those trailherds came from which they drove no one knew or asked. They moved like shadows on the Llano Estacado, here today and gone tomorrow, not seen for half a year, then reappearing as if they had not been away.

They seemed in rather poor case now, as if much had depended on that herd aimed for Abilene and so much of which had been lost en route. So Johnny nodded to Tim Coles, the bartender, and neither Frank nor Stron nor any of their men could pay for anything, and the tempo of the Silver Tip stepped up sharply. They put new liquor on top of that already taken on at the Lone Star, and soon the Silver Tip was roaring with laughter, with wild songs of trail and prairie, with the beating of heavy whiskey glasses on the bar. They yelled and stamped their hard-worn boots and made what passed for happiness in men of their kind and time and place.

And presently they sat in at the games, a trigger-hung

outfit, reckless and dangerous, and won or lost as straight luck decreed, backed by long experience. But wild as their men were, neither Frank nor Stron showed evidence of drink. Hard men, they could take and hold hard liquor with an amazing ease. Stron played poker with a sharp zest, but Frank leaned against 'he bar, his boot heel over the rail, and talked with John y Velantry. Their speech, quiet and careful, covered a thousand square miles and the scattered settlements in them as easily as folk of a less new land covered their farms, their towns, their counties. These men talked of an empire. They talked of trails and fords and established springs, of the western-moving buffalo, of cattle, and of grass. Always of grass, for on grass alone the life of the empire rested.

"Things are gettin' crowded, Johnny," Frank said. "Heard on th' Washita that the Porter boys, Buck and Pete and Ansell, are fixin' to run a stage line south from Abilene as far as Pond Creek, though who'll ride on it seems a question to me, considerin' that th' freighters carry folks that want to go south."

Velantry looked up quickly. "Why, that's fine," he said. "It will bring folks into the country, open it up, sort of."

But Frank Daunce frowned and his little topaz eyes were troubled. "Not to me it ain't fine," he said; "too many folks comin' in to th' Llano Estacado now. John Chisum's moved his whole outfit clear over west to th' foot of th' Capitans so's he'd have more room to run his stock. And with Jesse Chisholm makin' a bigger drive this year than last, clear from Red River north to Abilene, more an' more folks is goin' to get interested in the cattle industry."

"There's money in it, Frank," Johnny said. "Big money. Look at the tycoons already fat and getting fatter, scattered over this great range."

"Tycoons is right," Frank answered. "Th' big man, th' rich man. Money makes money. But the little rancher, th' poor man with a small, building herd, he's another matter. I begin to see the end of the little man."

Velantry threw down the cigar he was smoking, ground it in the sawdust with the heel of his soft black boot. "I do, too," he said. "I've already seen it, Frank. Right here, not a month ago." There was a bitter coldness in his voice; his face was harder than that of the man beside him.

"It's the time of the big man. But with people drifting into the country west of Abilene," he said, "there'll be more and more little men, and after a while there'll be laws, and less and less small herds will be drifted away with the big ones on the beef drives. Maybe it'll be the end of the big man as we know him now—a boss, a king, a baron whose word is law for a hundred miles each way around him. It's the end of the little man, Frank, for sure—unless there's a lot of them."

The other moved his elbows from the bar and shook his head. "I hate th' tycoons," he said cryptically. "They was made to be picked, if you're smart enough to do it."

Velantry's black eyes, scanning the room before him, did not waver, but in those words he had the answer to the Daunce boys, their comings and goings in a thousand miles of range, their disappearances and returns, their lean times and their affluence. It was something which he'd thought he knew, but its confirmation put into him now a strange sense of satisfaction, a filing away of information for that future which no man could foresee.

The Daunce boys had dark power. The power of complete cupidity coupled to a reckless courage, cougar-fierce, cougar-careless of the final outcome. To gather gold to spend for nothing worthy, these two men of the lawless places would risk their all, which was usually only life.

Johnny Velantry's face still held that hardness which the conversation had brought there, but behind his blank eyes fixed on the room a whirl of thoughts was racing, grim thoughts bridging past and future. For a long time he stood so, silent, withdrawn. Then he turned and touched the faded sleeve of the man beside him.

"Frank," he said, "I'd like a word with you. Let's get out of here for a little while. Can do?"

Frank Daunce glanced swiftly at him, nodded. "Can do, Johnny," he said mildly. "Anything you say."

They passed down along the bar, through a door at the back, and into that bare, clean place which Velantry called home. Here there was a table, a shelf which held a kerosene lamp, a dog-earned book or two, a bunk bed, and several chairs. It was barren of all comfort, but this man, fastidious as he was, could do without comfort. Now he laid aside his wide hat, drew a chair toward the table, motioned Daunce to another, sat down, and laid his clasped hands on the boards before him.

Sitting so he studied Frank's face a long moment before he spoke.

Then quietly he began to talk, and for twenty minutes there was no other sound in the room. Not once did Frank Daunce interrupt him. When he had finished, this man, shady of background, spendthrift of personal safety but ready for the long chance always, knew more about him than any man west of the Mississippi; but he had the stillest tongue also, and Velantry had no misgivings.

"This may be a bargain, Frank," he said quietly, "or it may be just a conversation. It all depends on what the summer tells me. At any rate you'll not be a loser either way, and here's what says so."

He reached into a breast pocket, drew out a flat packet, and took from it a sizable amount of money. This he pushed toward Daunce, who picked it up casually.

"Whichever it turns out to be, Johnny," Frank said quietly, "you can count on us."

"I'm sure of that. I guess that's all."

The two men rose and left the little room, went back

into the smoke and noise of the Silver Tip, and both were committed to something neither had dreamed of an hour back.

The night roared itself away, and in the gray dawn the Daunces and their men went out of town. Most of them were drunk, filled with a spurious happiness that spent itself in a chorus of yells, a burst of harmless gunfire. One thing they did. They stopped en masse beside the horses of the Fingermarks and looked their fill at those beauties, moving restlessly after long hours at the hitch rail.

Spink and Farloe, whose trick it was at guard, lounged silently beside them. Neither moved a finger, but their right hands hung down along their thighs. Every man who worked for Big Red, who took his extravagant pay, was bound to the Double K with a peculiar allegiance which included the risk of life and limb if need be. How much of this was due to the dynamic and amazing man himself, how much to their unspoken devotion to Copper Ann, no one could say. At least a part of it stemmed from their fierce, protective pride in the Fingermarks themselves.

So now these two watched the trail men with alert and hostile eyes, ready for the slightest move. But no one made that move. Only Frank and Seastron sat their rail-thin mounts, their dark hands crossed on their saddle horns, and drank their fill of these horses whose like they had never seen, but of which they had heard rumors as far south as Red River.

No one spoke, and after a while the strangers reined away and trotted out of town, headed down the furrow mark toward the Chisholm Trail and the decimated herd on which the Daunces had pinned such high hopes a month or so ago. Frank, who always rode ahead, carried with him an opulent sense of well-being due to the packet inside his shirt, the mental picture of a possible future. He smiled in his scant brown beard, his narrow topaz eyes were lighted with their old excitement at the prospect of gain, of danger. These things were meat and drink to the two brothers. They had cut their teeth upon them. They would probably dig their graves with the same tools.

A little later the Kincaid riders came out of the Lone Star Palace, ready for the ride home, the day's work that would surely follow the night's roistering. Big Red was not with them, and Sloan, on Skimmer, sat in the shadow of the blacksmith shop to wait until he appeared alone from the willows by the bridge to mount Streaker and take out after the others like an arrow from a bow. Then he came into the road behind him and set the Skimmer running, too.

And the cow town lay hushed and still behind them all, once more drained and dry of life.

Chapter Seven

JOHNNY VELANTRY WENT OFTEN TO HIS NEW HOLDING OUT
beyond the Little Willow Creek. He saw to it that Sam
Bolin was well provided with the necessities of life and
some of its more vital things, as Sam saw them, namely
tobacco for his pipe and a weekly bottle of the Silver Tip's
finest. And Sam, thus relieved of all responsibility, began
to swear by his boss to such chance riders as came by the
lonely cabin now and then.

"Finest feller I ever saw," he opined largely. "Open-
handed as all get out. An' he ain't scared o' nothin'. Took
a he-man t' beat Big Red to th' draw that day in town. Yes,
by jingo! An' just t' buy th' Silver Tip an' stay here! Becuz
Red ain't done with him, you c'n bet yer boots."

He gave this opinion seriously to Velantry himself, and
the other took it as seriously, a fact which raised him yet
higher in Sam's good graces.

"Don't treat a feller like he wuz a bum, jest becuz he's
a rifleman an' ain't settled in some place with prop'ty
an' such. No, sir!"

And bit by little bit Velantry began to question him.

"You been long around these parts, Sam?" he wanted
to know one day, sitting his horse in the cabin's yard.
"Know much about the different ranchers?"

"Wal," Sam answered judicially, "yes an' no. I ain't to
say a tethered man. Never wuz. I come an' go. Seen a heap
of this world, I have, Johnny. Been from Abilene clear over
to th' edge of th' Rocky Mountains, east and west, an' from
here south to th' Canadian Bottoms. Sure am a traveled
feller."

Velantry nodded soberly. "About how long you been traveling this country?"

"Oh, mebbe twenty–thirty year."

"Then you saw the buffalo leave, the cattle crowd in."

"Sure did! An' them wuz th' days, too, Johnny. I mind me Hank Davis, up northwest of Blue Buttes, when he druv in six thousan' head an' settled on th' Black Snake Creek. He——"

"You see Kincaid come in?" Velantry cut in casually.

Sam brushed back a strand of his grizzled brown hair with a vain sweep of a dirty hand.

"Not eezackly," he said. "You see, there was a woman south on the Llano Estacado—a Arapaho, she wuz, an' purty as a shiny brown chipmunk—an' I'd been down in them parts fur quite a spell. Let's see. That wuz in fifty-three. Mebbe fifty-four. But when I hit these parts agin— they wuz a young Arapaho buck wanted that brown girl, too, an' I had to leave out of there right pronto. Seemed best— well, when I got back north here, Big Red was already here an' settled in. Had most of th' house an' barns on th' Double K already built an' cattle scattered over six hundred acres. Longhorns, they wuz, th' great-granddaddies of his present herds, an' he'd come in from Texas. That was long, long before Jesse Chisholm blazed th' Trail, which ain't but two years old now, as everybody knows."

"Yes," Velantry said with a certain softness in his voice, "that was a long time back. Fifteen years ago. He's prospered, it seems."

"Yep," Sam said, "he has. In lots of ways. Some of it fair an' square. Some like Bill Smith an' Elvira. They ain't th' only ones. There was th' Jount boys, Hez an' Horace, over due west. Had a sizable herd, but they wuz cleaned one night, complete. Gunfire, too. When th' smoke cleared away an' someone rode by next day there just wasn't any Jount outfit. Both Hez an' Horace was deader'n doornails, an' all their riders gone, vamoosed, scared right outen th' country. Nobody knew anything about th' whole affair. But th' Kincaid ranch druv next day. Took their beef over towards th' Indian Territory where they used to be traders come in an' buy stock, take their chances of gettin' through to th' states east. Many's th' outfit them days, over yon, that lost all they had, includin' theirselves. Raiders used t' stand 'em agin trees an' use 'em for practice purposes, an' sometimes even th' traders what was supposed to buy jest took. Yes, siree, them wuz th' days."

Later Velantry's quiet probing passed over and beyond Sam, although with a good memory and in his pay Sam gave him the best picture of those early days. In a land where all question of a man's past was strictly taboo, Velantry had to use consummate care in the rebuilding of that past.

But rebuild he did, and always it was one man's past, one man's ways, one man's prospering. Little by little and bit by bit, from this far rider and from that, he gleaned his ancient news.

Yes, it was a fine country, with plenty of opportunity for those who had the brains and the guts to grab the same. Sure, many men had, still were doing so. Hard work, of course. Especially for the little man with a few half-wild cattle under brand. Eternal vigilance, and sometimes failure. Of this latter and more-than-even chance, no one had much to say. The memory of the Jount boys, even so far back, was still fresh in the stockmen's memories, and there was Bill Smith of this day. So Velantry skirted that aspect, too.

But how about the man who came here with money of his own to start?

Oh, they told him, that was a horse of another color. Money to build, to buy Texas cattle and drive them north to this virgin grassland, to see them multiply; money to hire help. Yes, that was something else. Especially to hire help that could be depended on. In such circumstances a man

—most any man—could prosper, could become rich, a cattle king in his own right.

But few men, Velantry held, brought money to the frontier, could afford to start that way. He doubted if there were any around here so fortunate. Indeed, he'd seen no one who gave him that impression.

No? they asked him. Well, of course—no offense, Johnny —of course he was a newcomer, a tenderfoot, and couldn't be expected to know. But there was Hanson of the Circle H, southwest on the Llano's edge, who'd been well heeled when he came in, a cattle baron now. And there was Red Kincaid, right here on Bent Bow Creek.

Kincaid? Velantry asked. Was Kincaid rich, too, on arrival?

Sure, they told him. Not lousy rich as he was now, a power and a rolling force, but with enough to set himself up in style in the very first year.

So the probing and the building went so quietly ahead that those who spilled old knowledge never knew they were being drained. And presently the widely scattered questions ended, for the picture stood complete. The time, the man, his methods, his ferocious courage under opposition—all these things held established places in it.

But there was one thing that Johnny could not fathom, one question to which there was no answer, no matter how adroitly put or to whom.

No one in the country knew where Big Red came from. There was no trail behind him beyond the beginning of that first long drive up from south Texas with his new-bought herd of longhorns, his wife and small girl child. He might have dropped from Heaven, so far as any person knew. No one had ever asked, and Big Red had never said.

So there was a blank spot in the pattern which the young man with the gambler's hands, the unreadable black eyes, was so slowly and carefully weaving. But it could wait. Someday it would be filled, the tapestry be finished. .

And so Johnny Velantry entered into the second phase of the thing which had stopped him in his wanderings, held him in this tiny frontier town. The wide net of his purpose drew in to narrower confines and its center was Big Red Kincaid. And with that narrowing, small clouds of portent no bigger than a man's hand began to drift across the horizon of his life. Danger like his own shadow drew in behind him. He knew it was there. It was no stranger. For three full years it had companioned him potentially, but always tentatively, in the background. Now he sensed it a little in the open, a bit more bold. Well, he'd asked for it, invited it along. And it had an effect upon him, steadied his always steady hands to a machinelike precision, sharpened his keen sight, his hearing, stepped up the whole live tempo of his being.

He sent out with Ben Alverson's freight teams for new and better clothes from Abilene, replenished the Silver Tip's stock of liquid refreshment with liquor so smooth that men smacked their lips in new pleasure, held his glasses to the light to see its jewel-like brilliance, its clarity.

"You sure know how to do things, Johnny," they told him gracefully. "The Tip's gettin' to be the best saloon in town."

That speech got back to Red Kincaid and set him into a raging fury. He swore for an hour straight on end and vowed he'd buy the Silver Tip, lock, stock, and barrel. Kincaid ways, Kincaid possessions, had been too long the top of the pack for him to take kindly to anything or anyone which threatened that supremacy. And Copper Ann, listening to his tirade, shut her lips primly and agreed to every word. What threatened Big Red in any way was wrong to her—had always been, still was—and the sooner he ousted this outlander in the dandified black clothes the better.

"You do that, Red," she told him across the supper table, "and I'll deal faro for you. I'd love the job."

"All right," Red answered. "That's all I need. If you want to run that layout, I'll see you get it."

She laughed with an arrogance to match his own, but for once the men around the table were silent.

"That ain't no place for you, Ann," Ennis Sloan said deliberately, "an' you know it. You know it too, Red."

"Who's to say it ain't," Kincaid asked sharply, "if I say it is, and my girl says it is?"

"Th' talk of th' town, that's who," the foreman said doggedly. "There's plenty already, with her playin' at the Lone Star, let alone dealing at th' Tip."

"Hell! Woman's talk. Don't amount to a hill of beans. Women would talk about her if she didn't do anything but walk along the street, just if they got one look at her." There was ineffable pride in his voice. "You don't hear the men talk about Copper Ann Kincaid."

Sloan fell silent, but disapproval was heavy in his silence and in that of the men around him. The girl was on a pedestal and they didn't want it shaken. No one could press his luck too far. Not even the Kincaids themselves.

But Big Red was used to pressing luck, and later in that week Johnny Velantry was asked to sell the Silver Tip. The freighter, Ben Alverson, came in and leaned against the bar, toyed with a glass of the fine whiskey his wagons had brought a few days previously, and put the matter straight.

"How'd you like to go out of the saloon business?" he asked. "Sell out for cash—lock, stock, and barrel?"

The other looked at him quickly, but there was little or no expression on Alverson's face.

"Who wants to know?" Velantry said mockingly. "I didn't know you belonged to Big Red, Ben. Thought you were an independent wagon man."

The big man's features did not change. He shook the liquor around in his 'glass, regarded it profoundly, and Johnny tried again.

"Maybe you don't," he said, still in that mocking tone.

"Maybe it's the girl. Maybe it's Copper Ann you belong to."

At that Alverson looked up, and his eyes were cold as Northern Lights. "Maybe," he said with deceptive softness, "there's a good many men north of the Llano who belong to Ann. And she usually gets what she wants—anything she wants. Maybe she wants the Silver Tip."

At the insolent and unveiled threat a surge of anger boiled up inside Velantry. "There usually comes a time," he said, "when even the most spoiled brat fails to get what it wants. This is one of them. I bought this place because I wanted to own and run it. I still do. And you can tell the Kincaids —both of them—I mean to do just that."

Alverson straightened up, set down his glass, still half full. "You had your chance," he said. "If business falls a little slack you can blame yourself. So long."

"If business is too scared of the Double K outfit to come into my place," he said hardily, "why, I'll give it—lock, stock, and barrel—to Stella Adams. As an alternative to your offer, it would be a pleasure."

Alverson, who had turned away, whirled on his heel, his face black with sudden fury, but his action was a little late. Velantry's right hand was inside the new black coat, his eyes were narrow. The other looked at him a long moment, licked his lips, and walked stiffly from the room.

Dead silence followed his departure, for thirty men had heard the sharp-cut words. Then here and there a small group rose, cast in its hands, set down its drinks, and followed Alverson, until more than half of them had left the Silver Tip. Those who remained sat or stood where they were for a strange, still moment. Then a man over beyond the faro table laughed.

"First time in seven years!" he said shrilly, "that anyone's stood up against th' Double K! Deserves a drink all round! Set 'em up, Johnny, on me."

Velantry drew a long breath, removed that telltale hand,

and a boyish grin replaced the hardness on his face. "Maybe
it does, at that," he said. "But it'll be on the house. Better
take it while you can. Might not be any house a little later.
You heard what Ben said."

The men, most of them of the town itself—the barber,
the blacksmith, Mead of the general store which Kincaid
did not own, and others—came up to the bar and soberly
raised the glasses which the bartender as soberly filled. It
seemed, somehow, a small ritual, a repudiation of old
things, a welcoming of new. Velantry drank with them.
They set down the empty glasses and looked at him with
speculative eyes.

"Johnny," Mead said, "we know how fast you are on th'
draw from that day you brought in Elvira Smith. But
you're only one. You got to have eyes in th' back of your
head from now on. Big Red's bossed this country a lot too
long to let anyone stand against him if he can help it—
and he'll have lots of help."

"I know it, Ves," Velantry answered, "but a man's got
only one life to live and he's got to live it as seems best to
him. I've made a stand here in this town, and it seems best
to me to—stand. I aim to do so, Kincaid or no Kincaid."

"By——!" Sylvester Mead said harshly. "I wish you'd
come here long ago. A few good men—poor men—might
still be alive, might be running their herds. And a lot of
others might be more able to say their souls are their own.
We've taken a lot and just stood back. Been pushed back.
Like a bunch of sheep without a bellwether. Big Red's
word has been th' law. Maybe, just maybe, if we had a
bellwether we might herd up against him. Looks like we
got one. What you say?"

"I say you're dam' right, for one!" Doak Haynes, the
blacksmith, said, and others backed him up.

Velantry stood for a while considering, his eyes on the
floor. Then he looked up and carefully scanned the faces
of these men. One by one he placed them, and all had

stakes to win or lose in any stand against the Double K outfit. But he had played a lone hand always. It did not suit
him now to do otherwise.

"Thanks, boys," he said presently, "but if the trouble
which seems to be in the offing for me develops, as it likely
will, it could well draw some of you, maybe all of you, into
it, too. I wouldn't want that. I mean to stay here, to keep
the Silver Tip, and to go on the way I've started. If any of
you feel you are on my side of the fence, all well and good.
I'll be glad of that. But don't make an issue of me or anything that might happen to me. You got no call to do so.
But it's good to know there are so many of us think alike."

"All right, Johnny," Sylvester Mead said slowly. "If you
don't want to make a faction of us behind you, why, that's
your business, but you can't stop us being there anyway. On
your side of the fence. We been a long time on th' other
side from Red as it is."

"Too dam' long," the blacksmith said. "A bunch of
coyotes with our tails between our legs."

"Not quite that bad, Doak," Hilmer, the barber, cut in.
"Most of us've got families. I'd hate to see my wife a widow
just because I'd bucked a losing game."

"That's right," the other answered soberly. "Bill Smith
was married."

"Well, anyway," Sylvester summed it up, "maybe we'll
all stand a little closer to our mark now Johnny's set a
better one."

"Will so," Doak Haynes said, nodding. "Just will so."

And so the matter rested for the present.

But it did not take long for Velantry's refusal to sell the
Silver Tip, and the manner of that refusal, to begin to bear
its fruit. The very next week, when the Alverson freight
train pulled into town, no wagon drew up before Mead's
store. Sylvester, waiting for a consignment of salt and calico,
sugar, slickers, shoes, boots, and blankets from the East,
went down to the freight corrals to find Ben. He found him

busy looking over the stock and wagons, talking to his drivers, most of whom would push on over west with morning, for the Alverson wagons hauled far into the hinterland of tiny settlements and scattered ranches.

"Ben, what in th' world?" Mead said anxiously. "Where's my goods?"

"Why, how'd I know?" the freighter answered, grinning. "I ain't seen any goods of yours."

Mead looked at him in utter astonishment.

For five years Ben Alverson had done all the hauling from Abilene for Mead's Emporium. He knew as much about that end of Mead's business as Mead did himself. It was incredible. For a moment more the storekeeper stood in puzzled bewilderment, and then it flashed upon him.

"I see," he said slowly. "I'd never have believed it of you, Ben. You've been as square a man as there is around this country. And it's not Big Red, either. Not directly. Your men could handle his. No. Velantry must have been right. It's Copper Ann."

Alverson's mouth set hard, and he jerked at the strap he was fixing on a broken hame. "You leave Ann alone," he said harshly.

"Oh, shut up," Mead said disgustedly. "Stop acting like a fool. You're old enough to know better. And th' whole range's got a right to speak of Ann. She's part of it, as much as any man. We all know she's a good girl, but she's no angel, so don't ride your high horse because a man calls th' turn on you and her. It sticks out all over you. Wonder I never noticed it before—an' you old enough to be her father! Well, I suppose you're through hauling for me—or anyone else who don't lick Big Red's boots. So be it." And he turned and went angrily back into town. He went direct to the Silver Tip.

"Johnny," he said, "it's started. Alverson deliberately left my freight in Abilene. Won't haul another pound for me. That means you, too, of course. We'd better get hold of

Shally soon as possible. He's a little string, only three wagons, but he'd like our business. He hauls south to Caddo Springs, an' is longer between trips, but he'd be glad to come around this way to have our trade. He's due next week."

"Fine," Velantry said. "I told you, Ves, and I'm sorry. . . . But we'll make out," he added stubbornly. "No man can run a world, no matter how small a one, forever. He's bound to reach his match sometime. We'll match Kincaid and Alverson, too. Though I'm sorry Ben's in this. He seems a right square man."

"He is—or has been—but you were dead right when you twitted him about Ann. It's her, all right. Got mad as hell when I said the same just now. Funny how that redheaded girl can twist any man she picks around her little finger. Just so funny it ain't."

"It's old as Adam, Ves," Velantry said, smiling. "You know what Eve did to that poor guy—and all the rest of us. A beautiful woman is the sharpest weapon in this world. . . . How do we get hold of Shally?"

"Just go out and meet him on th' Trail. He'll follow the Chisholm straight down. I'll send out a scout to wait for him and come and tell us, then we'll go. 'Bout four days from now, I figger. And, damn it, Johnny, we'll have to offer a stiff freight rate to make sure of him. He'll know, once we lay our cards on th' table with him, what he's likely to face about th' second trip, when Ben finds out he's taken over for us."

"That's all right with me. Part of the game."

"Yes. 'Tis so. Just the beginning. Well, so long."

Chapter Eight

THE FIRST BIG TRAIL-HERD WAS COMING UP THE CHISHOLM.
It had been gathered beyond the Canadian Bottoms by
men as tough as the mounts they rode or the raiding
Comanches they encountered, and it was following the
new grass north. It was about ten days behind that poor
remnant which the Daunce brothers had brought up, and it
heralded the important drives of the summer to follow. It
spread across the landscape like a monstrous mottled blanket, articulate with monotonous bawling, slow-moving as
a lava stream and as relentless. Its head moved into the
green land, its drag sent up tall clouds of dust where the
churning hoofs destroyed all living things.

The herds to follow would be wider spread, deployed on
either side of the Trail to find that forage without which
no beef drive could be made, for these vast hordes of longhorns literally ate their way from the Llano Estacado to
Abilene and the rails that would take them east and to
oblivion. Week after slow week, creeping up the plains,
they marked an era as wild and free and lonely as the world
has ever known. They stood for progress, hotly as the
men who drove them would have resented any thought of
change, and with them rode hardship and danger, ruthlessness and skill, and a certain brand of romance. They covered only a few miles daily, and behind them followed the
remuda, the horses of the outfit. Along their outer fringes
the cowboys rode, at lead and point and drag, and their
voices rose in the almost constant singing which was so
much a part of the scene. Songs of cow camp, plain, and
settlement—ribald, sentimental, sometimes harking back

to the battlefields of Shiloh, Gettysburg, and Bull Run, or to some quiet little church in a forgotten childhood. Weary of the daylong march, the cattle bedded down at night to chew their sweet cuds and drowse away the starlit hours, the men unsaddled, turned their horses into the remuda to be replaced next day with fresh ones, and ate ravenously around the fires and the chuck wagons.

And somewhere up ahead there was waiting that plowed furrow, dotted with its monuments of sods, which led away toward a tiny frontier town and such pleasures as it might afford. And the town was waiting for them, swept and garnished, stocked with liquor and the "store food" so much prized by men long accustomed to coffee, beef, and biscuits—namely, dried apples, raisins, rice, salt pork. The Blue Top's cooking pots would boil all day, its oilcloth-covered tables never long empty. Mothers kept their children off the street, young women were filled with hidden excitement, for when the trail men hit the town it usually blew wide open and anything could happen.

They hit it late one afternoon when the sun was well down along the early summer sky, twenty-two of them, lean and hard and many frankly ragged, though clean as sun and wind on bush-spread garments could make them, dark from those same elements, already building with inner excitement.

They came in yelling like Comanches, preëmpted the first hitch rail, tramped into the first saloon, which was the Lone Star Palace. Like the Daunce crowd they proceeded first to try to drink the bar dry, and Big Red's good liquor soon raised their starved spirits like a stream in a spring freshet. Whooping with laughter they crowded the card tables, threw away their money on the roulette wheel, slapped friend and stranger on the back alike, and the first of the summer's periodic jamborees had begun. The trail boss had promise them two nights and a day, and they meant to waste no minute of it. In the next six hours they would almost take the place apart—almost, not quite, for the Double K outfit was already there—drink themselves into the sawdust by morning, and sleep like the dead until around noon, when they would waken as if nothing had happened and proceed to do it all over again.

And so they did. And all of it inside the Lone Star Palace. But a new day was a new day, and here and there a man roused, sat up, wiped his face with a soiled hand, and began to look around for food. He roused his fellows, yelled, "Breakfast, boys! A white man's breakfast! Come o-n-n-n an' get it!" And they rose with all the dignity of a slept-off drunk and marched solemnly into the Blue Top for that rare treat, a woman-cooked meal with raised wheat bread, stewed apples and, wonder of wonders, all the fresh eggs they could eat.

After that they were ready for anything, any new worlds to conquer.

They wiped their long mustaches on the backs of their hands, hitched up their lean-bellied belts, settled their shooting irons comfortably on their thighs, and sallied forth. They stood together in the street and looked over the meagre stretch of buildings, counted the saloons, and proceeded to take them in line. The first one beyond the hotel was the Silver Tip, and they headed for it in a body. But along the hitch rail in front of it a line of cowmen like themselves leaned comfortably, affable smiles on their faces.

"Howdy, boys," Ennis Sloan said pleasantly. "How you find your breakfast?"

"Howdy," the trail boss answered. "Fine. Best dam' meal any of us've had sence we left Rush Springs. Yes, better'n that one. They didn't have no aigs. Where'n hell do you git aigs up here?"

"At th' Double K," Ennis said. "Our boss, he owns th' Blue Top an' the Lone Star an' about half this here town.

He aims to treat th' trail men right on every count, even down to eggs. Raises his own hens out to the ranch."

"Be dam'!" the other said. "Must be a fine feller. What's his name?"

"Big Red Kincaid."

"No wonder. Heard of him two–three year back. Big cattle tycoon, ain't he?"

"You bet," said Ennis. "And if you boys want th' best liquor in town, th' straightest games, w'y th' Lone Star's th' place."

"Yeah, but we done went all through it last night. Like to try 'em all," the other said reasonably. "We ain't overlookin' no bets."

He looked up at the neat front of the Silver Tip, its spruce new sign.

"Looks like a right nice place," he said. "Guess we'll give it a try."

Ennis Sloan straightened from the hitch rail. "Just a minute," he said in a low voice. "We'd advise against it."

The trail boss, still a bit important with last night's well being, swayed a little. "An' why, might a feller ask?" he said mildly.

"Well, for one thing," Sloan said, "we don't consider th' liquor in here any too good. Ain't none of us will touch it. An' we don't feel th' games are straight's they might be. We don't——"

The half-cut swinging doors of the Silver Tip swung open, and Johnny Velantry in his elegant black garb stood there, his eyes on Sloan's face.

"You don't what, Sloan?" he said thinly. "Don't own this place? Won't share the Trail's trade with any other saloon? Because Big Red owns half the town and the country, must he have all the rest?" The black eyes, alight with anger, swept to the trail boss, the men behind him. "Gentleman," Velantry said gracefully, "I own the Silver Tip,

and if you'll step in the place is yours scot free for the first
hour. All the drinks you want, and you be the judge of
their quality. Is that a fair deal?"

"Fair deal?" the trail boss said instantly. "Mister, it's four
aces every way! I consider that right handsome. Come on,
boys, let's go."

The crowd swung round the hitch rail and the men who
stood there.

"Aigs or no aigs," the boss grinned as he passed Sloan,
"we can't turn down an invite like this."

But Sloan, whose eyes had missed nothing in the noon-
day street, put out a hand. "Wait a minute, pardner," he said
evenly. "Take a look yonder."

The other, his booted foot on the first step of the Silver
Tip's porch stairs, stopped where he was and looked back
up the street.

Ann Kincaid in her trim green habit, her head like copper in the sun, rode up before the Lone Star on Stormwind
and sat a moment while the stallion breathed and blew
and shook himself. She leaned forward to pat the arched
silver neck and slid gracefully down.

The man from the Canadian Bottoms took his foot from
the step and licked his lips. " 'Tain't so," he said aloud,
wonderingly. "It just ain't nowise so!"

"Is so," Sloan answered with a savage pride in his voice.
"Is so. The boss' daughter, Miss Ann Kincaid, and th'
best gambler north of th' Rio Grande. She plays poker with
all comers at the Lone Star Palace. And she's a lady to her
boot heels. There's a hundred men round here who say so—
and let nobody forget it for a minute. Now, how'd you like
to play at th' Lone Star?"

Sloan moved, his own men behind him, and behind
them like bits of steel behind a magnet the whole crowd
from the Chisholm flowed away without a backward glance.
They had forgotten Johnny Velantry and his saloon, his
offer of everything free for a riotous hour. They had for-

gotten everything they ever knew with one sight of the gorgeous beauty of a slim girl in a green riding habit on a big blue horse.

With unconscious drama Sloan held them slightly back, until Copper Ann had tied her mount and go· ·up the steps and entered. Then, with a strange diffide: ·, these hard men from a hard way of life followed hei ·nto the Lone Star Palace. They stood in silence while she drew off her gloves, laid them on the bar's end, and passed down along it, her white hand sliding on the polished edge with that old seeming of delight in beauty, wherever found.

And back at his empty place Johnny Velantry stood with his face like a thundercloud. Here were the first fruits with a vengeance. Big Red and Big Red's men meant to ruin him, to drive him out of the country, and that he could accept, could understand. That they should use this girl— this "sharpest weapon"—to do the trick was inconceivable. But it was not a case of "they." Ann Kincaid herself was in on this, he knew instinctively. He heard it in the memory of her voice that day beside the creek, her spiteful words, "We don't like scrub stock on our range."

His eyes narrowed, thinking back.

She was her father's daughter. Like him. Like Big Red. Hard, ruthless, proud. Arrogant and vain. Like him, she and hers must be first in all things, brooking no opposition. Like him she would stoop to use any and all tools to gain her ends. Yes, Ann Kincaid, Copper Ann Kincaid, was surely Big Red's daughter!

And yet, there had been the day in the street when Bill Smith had been killed. He could still hear her cry, "Oh, Red! Did you have to?" There had been tears in her voice. He'd seen them in her eyes when he'd given her the gauntlet gloves to grip, to hold to. He'd pitied her then. Now he knew there was no cause for pity in her.

While he stood on his deserted porch Sylvester Mead

came across the dust of the street and climbed the steps to stand beside him.

"I know," he said. "I heard. Strike two. No freight. No customers. And all of us depend from year to year on th' trail men for our biggest profit. Th' rest of th' time we just make ⸱ t."

Vel⸱ ⸱ry nodded. "It was a clever trick, Ves," he said, "the girl's arrival. Sloan timed it right."

"Yeah," Sylvester said. "I think he sent for her this morning. Saw Bryce an' Farloe leave out about two hours back. Just about time."

"I thought so!" Velantry said violently. "Bait! Big Red's bait! She could ruin the town if her father set his mind to it. Every cowpoke in two hundred miles melts if she gives him one look from those long blue eyes of hers—and I think half the men in town are just as bad, married or single."

Sylvester reached up and pushed his hat back on his head. A grim smile touched his lips.

"You're half right at that, Johnny," he said honestly. "No man in his senses could look at Ann Kincaid and not feel his blood run hot inside him, no matter how much he might love the woman he's got. It's just nature an' there ain't any gainsayin' that. I b'lieve you followed her out of th' Lone Star yourself, th' first time you'd laid eyes on her, didn't you? Picked up the gloves she'd left on th' bar an' give 'em to her in the street?"

A flush, half anger and half embarrassment, flowed up along Velantry's face. "Yes," he said shortly, "I did. I don't know why I picked them up, but I do know why I gave them to her. I saw her fingers working when she saw what Red had done. It seemed she needed something to hold on to. Seemed lost, somehow."

"That's just it in a nutshell," Mead said, thinking. "Men want to touch something she's touched, like th' bar's edge where she always runs her palm along. Ever see fellers put their hands down on it like it was a woman's cheek? No,

I guess not. You ain't been in the Lone Star since that day, have you? Well, they do. And to hear the sound of tears in her voice—no man could stand it. But no one dared to do anything about it but you. You wouldn't either if you'd been here a little longer. No man touches Copper Ann."

"Sacred, is she?" Velantry said bitterly.

"Just about. In this man's country, anyway."

"Well, she's not to me. She's just—her father's daughter. By the way, where's Kincaid? I haven't seen him. Is he in town?"

"Sure," Mead said. "Where'd you suppose he'd be after a big night? Across the bridge, of course."

"You think the girl don't know?"

"Dam' right she don't. The whole town keeps it from her. They'd better if they don't want to keep Bill Smith company."

"Where are the Kincaid horses?" Velantry asked. "They're not around. Only her stallion."

"All in th' stable, out of sight. With too many men around town it'd take all hands from th' Double K to keep an eye on them. They're a temptation to any rider on earth. Almost as much as Ann herself."

"More, to me," Velantry said.

"Well, guess I might's well go on back. Don't suppose airy one of them fellers will come near my store. Buy everything they need in Big Red's place. This keeps up he'll run us both out of the country, Johnny."

Velantry shook his head. "He will not, Ves," he said soberly. "Not if we all stick together like we said. Maybe we'll run him out."

"Run out Big Red?"

"Yes. Big Red."

"You'll have to kill him, Johnny. He won't run."

"A skunk always runs, sooner or later, Ves. If not—well, we do kill skunks."

For a long moment Mead stood and studied the face of

the man before him. "Seems like," he said finally, "seems like—like Kincaid means more to you than anyone else. And you've known him less. I'm not asking, Johnny. I'm thinking."

The black eyes flashed up, and once again they were cold as dark waters. "Don't think, Ves," Velantry said softly. "Just don't think."

"No one can stop a man from havin' his thoughts," Mead said reasonably, "and I'll still have mine. But I don't have to express 'em. Not to anyone but you. I think, Johnny, that you know something of Big Red from away back."

Velantry studied him this time. He threw down the cigar that had gone cold in his mouth, put his heel upon it from long habit, the habit of a man who rides in prairie grass.

"I wish I did—know," he said cryptically. And then suddenly he said, "Ves, did you ever see Big Red with his shirt off?"

"With his shirt off? Hell, no! Why should I? He always comes in to town in his fine rider's clothes. I've never seen him at work. I fancy few have. Big Red takes life easy. He fancies himself a lot. Times was—ten, eleven year ago—when he did some fancy ridin' up and down th' street here, bareheaded and that red beard flyin', with the eyes of every woman in the place turning after him. That was before Stella Adams come in on a freight wagon and settled in her cabin. He's been tame ever since. But I reckon if anyone's seen him with his shirt off it's her. I'm sure wondering."

Velantry looked off along the creek where the willows had changed their soft spring green for the darker hue of summer, and his face was grave.

"Maybe," he said, "sometime you'll have no need to wonder. Just maybe."

The hours that followed were a strange interim. Inside the Lone Star Palace roaring, if oddly controlled, life filled the place. Men drank—and held their drinks. They played

and lost at poker, or won what Copper Ann allowed them
to win, for she could bluff out a royal flush on a pair of
deuces. They crowded around her table and took turns at
sitting in, and drank in her amazing presence with hungry
eyes.

And the girl was happy with them. Her blue eyes swept
them all impartially, her ready laughter made a music more
intoxicating than her father's liquor, while the long, warm
day drew by.

But presently she pushed up the shining curls on her
temples, wiped the palms of her hands together as if she
washed away the time, the place, the people, and rose to her
graceful height. She smiled at them.

"Gentlemen," she said in her clear voice, "it's been a
pleasure. I hope when you come up the Trail again you
won't forget us here."

"Ma'am," the trail boss said with true south Texas gal-
lantry, and a lot of truth, "we don't aim to forget you, ever."

"Thank you. And good-bye, boys. It's time for all good
girls to head for home."

She pushed in her chair, walked to the bar, smiled at
Curly, ran her hand along the polished edge, picked up her
gloves, and left the place.

As helplessly as water runs downhill they flowed out
after her, respectfully behind, and watched her reach for
Stormwind's rein, saw Bryce hold down a hand for her
booted foot and toss her lightly up.

But the stallion had stood too long at his end of the rail
with the strange horses, some of them mares, so short a
space removed, and he was in a sullen mood. He shook his
head and laid his ears back in the blowing foretop, and his
blue eyes flared in his silver face. The Double K men came
off the porch in a bunch but he was already back from the
rail, had jerked away from Bryce. Mostly Stormwind was a
pet, a friend, a well-used mount, but sometimes he was a
stallion to the broad heels above his iron shoes, and this

was one of them. The laid-back ears suddenly swung out from his head almost at right angles; he lowered his crest, opened his mouth, and bawled. The he charged headlong into the line of drowsing, hip-shot horses at the rail, and pandemonium broke loose. His teeth snapped at a lean flank and came away with a ribbon of skin. He lunged up by the forequarters and came down with his shod hoof striking, and his luckless victims plunged and screamed.

But the girl on his back was no one's weakling, no one's coward. She always carried, on a little built-in hook on the saddle's right side, a heavily leaded quirt, insurance for just this not-expected-but-possible thing.

She snatched it now and went into action herself. Grasping the whip by the thonged end of the leaded handle she brought it down between those outhung ears with manlike strength.

Again and again she cracked him down expertly, riding with consummate skill the mad cyclone which he had become, but without effect. Then she slid the whip through her hand and changed its ends and flailed his handsome white face, his tender muzzle, with the cutting thongs. That did the trick. Shaking his lowered head, blowing, still bawling, he backed out of the mass of terrified horses, turned east, and bolted like an arrow from a bow.

The riders of the Double K, racing for their own horses, meant to ride after her. The trail men stood in spellbound wonder at the girl's superb horsemanship. And beyond the blacksmith shop and Mead's store, Big Red Kincaid was just coming into the street from the willows by the bridge. No one breathed, watching, but all knew that if Stormwind merely ran Ann would ride him out to the end of his fury.

But it was not slated so. Just at the eastern end of town where the last house stood, Johnny Velantry was coming in on Ring. Once more he had been riding in the lonely world of prairie, creek, and thicket, thinking his dark thoughts, his hands crossed on the saddle bow. Now as the big blue stallion thundered down toward him he knew at once that something was wrong. The girl on his back was riding him, but she was not controlling him. He saw the out-thrust head, the peculiarly outhung ears, and knew the signs of stud horse fight. He swung the Ringer sharply out of the way to let this half-mad thing go by, but Stormwind swerved as he passed and his teeth snapped. They took a shred from the skirt of the fine black coat.

That swerve did something else. With the doubling strain of the big body, the back cinch of the sidesaddle broke, to flail around the horse's legs, and slowly the saddle began to turn. The girl had been thrown off balance. Now the horrified watchers saw her body begin to slide slowly down on the left side, saw her fighting desperately to cling to Stormwind's mane.

And they saw the rider on the chestnut horse fling him around, rising to pivot on his heels in a perfect circle, and lay him out full stretch along the dusty road. In the next few seconds they were to witness something no man among them would have believed. They saw the king of horses north of the Llano being slowly and surely overtaken by the slim brown streak from nowhere. They saw Johnny Velantry lean him to the left a little bit, saw him pull to Stormwind's streaming tail, his rump, his ribs, his quarter. Saw his rider reach out an arm and catch that clinging form in the green habit, hold it, racing alongside for a moment, then lean away and pull it free. For a breathless space they saw the man and girl, clinging together, ride out the chestnut's headlong speed, then slow and stop where the road turned round the bend of the willowed stream.

For a tight and awful moment these two remained in that embrace, the girl's slim body hanging down the Ringer's heaving side, her arms around Velantry's neck, his dark face bending down upon her shining head. His lips against the banded braids were sickly white. Then Ann tipped back her head and looked up at him with those long blue eyes between their copper fringes not six inches from his own. They were beautiful as the skies of Paradise, wide and deep and bewildered, like those of a frightened child, and once again the man felt that aching stab of pity, the need to steady the arrogant but shaking spirit in her.

"I have—no words," Ann Kincaid said, whispering, "no words—to thank you with."

For a heady and dangerous moment Velantry looked down at her, and some powerful, compelling force, outside his will and beyond his own volition, began to draw his lips toward that curved, half-open mouth.

Helpless as unleashed waters he felt himself bend to her. This was the power in the girl which all men knew and none resisted inwardly.

Then, as if a whip had lashed him, he straightened up, released his hold around her slender body, and slid her roughly to the ground.

"You need none, Miss Kincaid," he said coldly. "Scrub stock, horse or man, is beneath contempt."

And turning the Ringer sharply he rode back toward the running crowd coming along the street. At their head was Big Red himself. The man's face was a study. On it played the gamut of emotions—fear and horror and towering rage against the stallion, relief so great it was fantastic, and, beneath them all, chagrin against this man who was his benefactor. As they met he stopped uncertainly, looked up at Velantry.

"You saved my girl," he said bluntly. "Name any price in reason and I'll meet it."

Velantry pulled Ring to a spectacular halt. His dark face paled and hardened.

"Why, you—" he said through tight lips, "you bastard! Get out of my way!" and he swung the brown horse so close that it shouldered aside the boss of the town, the range, the country. Big Red stumbled back, swearing profanely. He shook a doubled fist at the rider's back and turned once more to where his daughter stood in the dust of the road beyond the bend.

Tension in the community heightened perceptibly.

Out at the Double K, Big Red Kincaid was all for killing Stormwind. He got his rifle from the house and tramped down to the barn where Buck No Shirt had stabled the horse when he came racing home without a rider. He'd even lost the sidesaddle somewhere on the way. But Ann ran down the path beside her father, her face as white as his, her anger just as hot.

"You will not, Red!" she cried, trying to catch the weapon. "You know what I've always told you! You do some evil thing like this, and I'll hate you to my dying day! I swear I will!"

As her beauty swayed other men, so this threat always swayed Big Red.

Now he slowed and faltered, set down the gun, which Ann promptly took, and shook his head.

"He almost killed you, girl," he said distressedly. "Someday he will do so—and then it'll be too late. I'll kill him then, but it will be too late."

"All right, you can then," the girl said firmly. "If I'm not here to ride him it won't matter, but as long as I live you let him alone."

"Then by——!" the man swore savagely. "You'll stay off his back! Don't you ever mount him again."

"Of course I'll ride him. If I can't—well, there just won't be anything, ever, on the Double K I'll want to do again. Stormwind is half my life—two-thirds of it."

They faced each other stormily, and something in them which was identical met and battled and fell back, and neither understood the other fully. For that matter Red had never understood this woman child he had raised and coddled and loved so passionately. That she could oppose him, could stand against his wildest rage without flinching, could face him down on any issue, had always amazed him. Now she had won again, just as she won at poker, with that determination to back up her bet showing in her face. Big Red shook his head again and turned away. Instantly she was after him, her hand on his arm.

"Don't take me wrong, Red," she said earnestly. "I love you. But I mean to live my life."

Chapter Nine

THE TRAIL MEN PULLED OUT AT DUSK AFTER A LAST GOOD MEAL at the Blue Top. With the spectacular departure of one slim girl in a green habit the town was suddenly empty.

And Johnny Velantry, frowning and depressed, rode out across the blowing grass toward the Little Willow Creek. There was a sullen anger in him. The last thing he wanted was any personal touch with the Kincaids, and that he had been placed in so vital a position toward them was a cause for anger. Toward Red Kincaid he was morally sure he had a fixed, unalterable objective which would affect his daughter, his possessions, his henchmen. He wanted nothing in this world to lessen by one iota the power of his drive toward that objective.

And now he had a memory which kept recurring. The heady memory of Copper Ann against his breast, the clasp of her young arms around his neck, the unbelievable beauty of her long blue eyes beneath those upcurled lashes.

"Damn!" Velantry said, and rubbed a hand across his face in the warm darkness.

He came finally to where the Little Willow made a bend around a meadow, dipped down and splashed across the shallow ford, and came up on the rolling prairie where the Smiths had made their small, doomed bid for life and happiness. The few buildings stood huddled close together, as if for protection against a hostile land, and they stood stark and quiet in the starlight. It was early evening, but there was no lamplight beyond the open door; the dog did not bark to greet him. He rode ahead slowly, wondering if Sam Bolin had gone to bed already. Perhaps. These old-timers of plain and forest lived by the sun, up with it at daybreak, to sleep with its setting. But the dog should have sensed his coming, at least. As he came in across the little flat there was the sudden sharp crack, the belching roar of a heavy rifle, and he heard the sinister whin-n-n-g of a bullet directly over his head.

"Sam!" he yelled, "Sam! Stop it! It's Velantry!"

"Well, I be dam'!" Sam Bolin hollered from the darkness of the little barn. The bar on the door scraped, the wooden swing-hinges squeaked, and the rifleman came out into the yard as Velantry rode up.

"What in thunder!" Velantry said violently. "You lost your mind?"

"Not to speak of," Sam said grimly. "But you jest about lost yours! I'd a-had your range in about another minute. Hell, Johnny, I'd hate like tunket to a-kilt you!"

"Well!" Velantry said. "That wouldn't be much help after you had. What's all this about?"

"Plenty," Sam said. "I ben beleaguered ever night for four days. Someone's ben around ever single one of 'em, a-snoopin' an' a-sniffin'. Shep's about had th' high strikes, but I ain't lettin' him out to do no chasin'. Don't want him shot. He's a good dog. First night they almost got th' pinto outen th' corral before I knowed they wuz around. Hadn't ben he's a right sensible horse he'd a ben out an' gone, but he jest stood there whilst someone was a sneakin' in to get him. Heerd a strange noise jest in time an' I let off ol' Betsy here, a mite high, like I done tonight. She speaks loud."

"I'll say she does!" Velantry said, laughing a little.

"But she aims true," Sam went on. "Can bust a acorn on a stump at ninety yard clean as a whistle. Well, as I was sayin', they's dirty work a-goin' on around here. Somebody's tryin' to scare me offen here an' take th' horse an' cow. Not that they're valuable, you understand. It's just part of somethin', I think. Somethin' agin you, Johnny. Prob'ly burn down th' whole place, once I'm scared off."

"H'm," Velantry said. "Yes, I think so too. I'm not

wanted in this country, Sam. And maybe I've no right to involve you in my troubles. Maybe you'd better give up and leave. There's little here of any worth. It's been—well, just part of a plan, too, to keep this place. My plan this time. A gesture, a thumb to nose, sort of. Want to pull out, Sam?"

The old man's eyes flashed in the darkness. He spat far out.

"Hell, no!" he said. "I ben on this frontier, man an' boy, fer twenty year, an' there ain't ben nothin' scared me offen anything. It's a pride with me, an' I'm too old to begin backin' out now. I don't aim to kill anyone, Johnny," he added earnestly, "but I don't aim to get bushwhacked neither. I mean to give fair warnin'. Two high shots, mebbe, an' if that don't have no effect—well, we'll know who's behint this thing anyhow."

"At least," Valentry said, "don't take chances yourself. I don't want you killed either. It would be on my conscience."

Sam Bolin looked up in the starlight. He could see in the dark like a cat. "You got one, Johnny?"

"No!" Velantry shot out harshly. "No, I haven't. And I don't want one. But that don't say I've got a right to let you get wiped out just to show something."

"You wouldn't have anythin' refreshin' in them big coat pockets, would you?" Sam asked guilelessly. "Gets a bit dry around here, seems like."

"Sure I have," the younger man said, grinning. "But maybe I'd better not leave it. You may need all your wits."

"Johnny," Sam said gracefully, "such wits as I've got merely gets sharpened up with likker. 'Specially good likker like you handle at th' Silver Tip."

Velantry reached in a sagging pocket and handed him a bottle. "Don't let it prove your undoing at last, Sam," he said. "And be careful. I'll be out again soon."

"I'm living in th' barn," Sam said. "Me an th' cow an'

old Paint an' Rover. Sort of a concen-trated community. I
can see all ways from th' loft. An' don't you worry about
this"—he held up the flask—"I'll take her in small install-
ments. Whiskey an' women's better that way."

Back in town, Velantry stabled the Ringer and lay for a
long time on his hard bed, thinking. Little things. Trying
to buy the saloon out from under him. Trying to destroy
the buildings on the homestead he had bought from Elvira
Smith. Trying to kill all trade at the Silver Tip. Little
things. And Big Red's plain hostility since the day he had
reached for his gun and Johnny had been quicker. There
was pride in Big Red. The swashbuckling pride of ownership, of wealth, of supremacy in the rangeland. Pride of
personality—the days when he raced the one street of the
town with his red beard flying that the women's eyes might
follow him. Pride in his daughter, his ewe lamb. Pride in
those ramping, heady, barren things, the horses of the
Fingermarks.

Was it because he, Velantry, had discounted all these
things before the men of the place that Big Red was so dead
set against him? Did he see in him a younger man, a man
quicker on the draw, a man who would not kowtow to
him in any way, that he must be rid of him? They were
small things. Too small.

Or did Kincaid see in him something remembered from
a long dead past? Was there in Velantry's face a resem-
blance to another face which he, Big Red, had once known
and since forgotten? Did the very look of him recall a
thing a man like Red Kincaid would deliberately forget?

Johnny sweated in the warm night and wondered how
it would be possible to see Big Red without a shirt. For
until he did, he would not be certain that this was the
man. The big man with red hair whom he had hunted
through the frontier's fringes for three years now.

If Kincaid was that red-haired man there would be on

his left breast, just above the heart, a red, peculiar scar. A scar made by a knife and shaped like a half moon with the points turned sharply down.

It was the sign-manual of a man's despair, an inept, futile stroke to even a bitter score, to mete out justice where there was no justice, a savage thrust against the world and all it held because of one who, in effect, was about to leave it. It would be an old scar, made eighteen years ago, in another time and place and way of life, and Johnny Velantry knew its description as he knew the back of his own hand.

If Big Red bore that scar he was the man, and Velantry meant to kill him. But he must be sure. Dead, certain sure. And he must not think twice of those long blue eyes beneath their coppery lashes.

So he turned on his side and slept, with Ring blowing softly in his stall behind the Silver Tip, the sounds from the almost empty barroom so thin they were nearly nonexistent. If Velantry's living had been entirely staked on his venture in the town he would be now in bad case.

But that, too, had been a gesture, a reasonable excuse to settle here that he might come to know his enemy.

And Red Kincaid was thinking, too. Long, uneasy thoughts that plagued him, with resentment for a younger man who was quicker on the draw and with something deeper, more disturbing. This was a vague, dim stirring in the limbo of the past, a moving of submerged, forgotten things which he could not remember, could not place, but which held the quality of ghostly footsteps echoing behind him.

Who was this stranger in his own domain? This daring and insolent man whose very presence constituted a challenge to Kincaid supremacy, Kincaid power? What was there about him which seemed so vaguely familiar, so dimly disturbing? Big Red did not know, but he meant to meet

that challenge and destroy it. If Velantry meant a final
showdown, so did Red Kincaid. These two thought in cold,
calculating terms.

But the girl out at the Double K thought in furious
humiliation. She lived again that awful moment when she
fought to cling to Stormwind's mane. She knew, none better, how little chance she had to escape falling beneath
those thundering hoofs. Good rider that she was, good
horsewoman, she closed her eyes in a certain cold horror
at the memory. And then she heard again the running feet
of the chestnut horse behind her, felt a strong arm slide
around her, pull her free, felt her own arms catch the
rider's leaning neck. In the cool dusk of the deep room she
felt again the strength of his lean body, his cheek against
her forehead. A vast wave of some new glory she had never
known flowed over her at the memory. She had looked up
at him shaken and bewildered, her resentment over what
he had done to Red forgotten in her gratitude, had whispered those humble words. And he had whipped her with
the lash of that harsh, "You need none. Scrub stock, horse
or man, is beneath contempt."

As he had humiliated Red that day in town before the
people in the street, so now he had humiliated her before
them.

Red Kincaid and Copper Ann. The two people in all
their little world who had never known defeat, whose ways
and works had been above reproach. Had been, but now
no longer were. She was filled with boiling anger at the
man who had brought this thing about. That he was young
—almost as young as she—and that there was a vital charm
about him she had felt before. Now she cast these things
from her consciousness, along with the harsh knowledge
that Big Red had been wrong when he killed Bill Smith,
and remembered only the coldness in Velantry's voice, the
contempt in his eyes.

The Kincaids. They had been always right. Maybe they were right still. Maybe Red had been right about Bill Smith.

At any rate they were of one blood and, as she had told him then, they would stand together always.

Next day Ben Alverson came out to the Double K. He drove a light buckboard and a pair of rangy duns, and he made somewhat of a figure even though the iron-gray wings above his temples, the lines in his handsome weathered face, plainly spoke his middle age. There were no men around, Red and his riders having gone early on some matter of the stock on the upper Bent Bow, and Ann met him on the veranda, cool and beautiful in a soft green dress that made her head above it stand out like gold. The man looked at her hungrily, and all that Mead had said of him concerning her stood out on his face. He was dead serious; he had been ever since he too had seen her slide from Stormwind's back.

"Hello, Ben," Ann said cordially, "good to see you. Come in and sit down."

She indicated one of the hand-hewn chairs and Alverson sank into it with the pantherlike grace which distinguished him. The girl, watching, smiled down at him.

"Ben," she said honestly, "I'll bet when you were young you were a handsome devil. Bet every woman in a hundred miles was in love with you. Weren't they?"

The man did not answer for a moment, and a slow red tide flowed up beneath his tanned skin. That "when you were young" had hit him like a blow between the eyes. It set so sharply forth the gulf between them. A gulf of time which he had, for three years now, refused to tolerate. Since Copper Ann was seventeen Ben Alverson had been in love with her, waiting until she should be a woman grown, capable of knowing her own mind, of seeing a man for what he was, of judging his stable worth. Now she was

so, and he would wait no longer. He had come here today
to tell her this, to watch her lovely face react to the knowledge, driven by the memory of that tragic moment in the
street. Driven, too, by the instinctive certainty that a
woman who owed her life to a man in so spectacular a
fashion as Ann owed hers to Johnny Velantry would be
dead sure to think about that man, perhaps to build around
him an aura of romance.

But the girl had innocently and unconsciously spiked
his guns before he could fire a single shot. He drew out the
makings and slowly rolled himself a cigarette. With the
first deep drag, the shock she had given him lessened. He
looked at her through the pearly smoke and smiled, his
dark eyes crinkling at the corners.

"Ain't that question a little brash, young woman?" he
wanted to know. "Wouldn't be digging into a man's past,
would you?"

"Don't have to." She laughed. "It sticks out all over you.
And yet, come to think of it," she added, "I don't recall
ever seeing you with any woman hereabouts. Never even
heard of you making up to one. You dance with all of us
at the dances, and you're a darn good dancer, too. How
come?" There was lively interest in her voice.

Here was, in a nutshell, handed to him on a platter, the
very opening he had come here hoping to create. All his
life he had recognized opportunity, taken it by the forelock.
He so recognized it now, though its approach had not been
all he could have wished. He leaned forward in his chair,
flipped away his half-finished smoke, and looked deeply
into her face.

"How come?" he said softly. "You want to know, Ann?"

"Sure I do," the girl said. "Wouldn't ask if I didn't,
would I?"

"All right. Here goes. I've been waiting for a girl to grow
up. A little, wild, tomboy girl with th' loveliest blue eyes in
all this world and a head like burnished copper. The only

one of her kind on earth and th' only one I ever cared two hoots about in all my life. Does that answer that question?"

Ann's lips fell frankly open and she stared at him, too dumbfounded to speak. Then she recovered herself.

"Why, Ben Alverson! You mean me?" she said.

"Is there any other blue-eyed, copper-haired girl around these parts? Any other Copper Ann Kincaid north of the Llano? Or south either?"

"Well, I'll be——" she said slowly.

"Hush. Don't swear."

He knew she could, on occasion.

Ann shut her mouth and swallowed. Alverson's face was very gentle, half sad, half exalted.

"Is it so strange, Ann?" he asked. "I know—the difference in age. You're twenty this very spring. I'm thirty-six. But there's something else between us, a little matter of love—worship I might say, Ann, adoration, whatever you might call the thing that's kept me from all women since I first laid eyes on you, a gangling, long-legged, brash young-un, four–five years ago last winter. For three of those years I've meant for this hour to come. So now you know."

He rose quickly, picked up his wide hat from the earth floor beside the chair, and set it sharply down over his right temple. He reached and took her hand, held it hard.

"Don't open your mouth," he said smiling. "Don't say a word. Just you do some thinking. Maybe in th' evening when the shadows of th' cottonwoods down yonder at th' Bent Bow come creeping up along the flat. So long."

It was a Mede-and-Persian law of the outfit, the town, the rangeland, that no man touched Copper Ann; but Alverson bent swiftly and kissed her on the lips.

Then he walked to the buckboard, picked up his lines, and drove away without a backward glance. Whatever the man was, had been, or would be, he was a consummate artist in this matter.

The girl stood where he left her, staring after him so

stupidly that she forgot to close her mouth, once more
open with astonishment. Then she fled to the sanctuary of
her own room and stood in its middle with her hot face in
her hands, shaken by emotions that warred within her, un-
bounded shock and wonder and humiliation. Her first kiss!
Her very first—and it had to be Ben Alverson! Old Ben
Alverson, good old Ben, but old Ben Alverson! She had
always liked him. He was her father's friend, of Big Red's
time and way and place in life, and she had accepted him
in that fashion, never cognizant of the fact that he was in
between Big Red and her. Kincaid was fifty-four. Ben was
thirty-six. She was twenty. Closer to herself than Red. Yes,
sure. And he was a man, a virile, graceful, handsome man.
And he was in love with her. With Ann Kincaid, whom no
man of the many who loved her hopelessly had dared to
tell, to touch, to kiss.

And now Ben Alverson had kissed her! Squarely on her
lips! A kind of despairful fury seized her, and she ran to the
shiny little commode where a washbowl stood beneath its
ornate pitcher, poured water, scrubbed her face, her hot
cheeks and her mouth. Mostly her mouth, as if by these
ablutions she could wash away the defilement of that first
male touch.

She began to cry a little, whimpering, and presently, like
always when her sheltered life took on some fancied hardness, the door opened softly and Little Fawn came in.

"H'm'm," the quiet, smart, brown woman said. "Man
again. New man?"

Ann whirled and flung herself at that ample breast.

"No!" she yelled. "No new man! Old man! And, oh—oh,
Fawn! He kissed me! Damn it! He kissed me!"

Little Fawn patted her heaving shoulder, smiling amus-
edly.

"Nem mind," she said comfortably, "nem mind. What
you expect? Think men look at you an' not want kiss you?
Mebbe someone, he got more guts than rest. He don' look

too long. He do. Won't be last time. Start now. More come. Other men kiss. No cry after while. Just laugh, mebbe. Mebbe kiss back an' go on 'bout you business. Mebbe some day man kiss an' sun, moon, stars, they all fall down, land in heart. Then no more other men. No more other kiss. No more cry. Come now. Wash face again. Come help me in kitchen. Men be comin' soon."

And once again Little Fawn had put the world back in its place.

Chapter Ten

A FEW DAYS LATER SHALLY'S FREIGHT WAGONS WERE RE-
ported coming down the Chisholm Trail, and Sylvester
Mead and Johnny Velantry waited for them where the
plowed furrow met that widely trampled scar that ran
across an empire's face. It was noon, and when the creeping
vehicles in their cloud of dust reached the spot they stopped
for parley with the horsemen and business was done around
the chuck rig where the cook set up a hearty meal. Mead
laid out the situation, asked Chad Shally to haul for him
and for Velantry. Shally, a little sandy man with mild gray
eyes, but known from Abilene to Red River as one of the
deadliest shots along the Trail, considered long and soberly.
He knew the Double K outfit by reputation, and that it
did not bear tampering with, but he was in the freighting
business. He had come into south Texas the year before,
broke and shabby, and had scratched together the small
outfit which he now ran from railhead to Red River, and
he needed all the hauling he could handle. At a profit, of
course, and now Sylvester Mead offered him profit beyond
his wildest dreams, but he offered him danger as well.

He finished four biscuits and two cups of coffee before
he spoke. Then, "I s'pose you know what you're askin',
Mead," he said, "an' I know what I'm takin' on. Th'
minute Kincaid hears about this deal—an' that'll be right
after I deliver your first load in town—he'll see to it I have
trouble a-plenty."

"I know that," Mead said soberly. "That's why I mentioned th' price I did. It's a stiff price, Chad, but Mr.
Velantry an' me, we just don't aim to let Big Red run us

out of business by cuttin' off our supplies if we can help it. Well, what you say? You game—an' able?"

Shally rose and dusted off the seat of his pants, wiped his long mustaches carefully with a red bandanna, nodded quietly.

"Yes, sir," he said mildly. "Both, I reckon. Two weeks from today I'll be comin' back up by here empty, an' you be here with your orders all made out proper, an' I'll do th' rest."

"Fair enough. We'll be here."

The loaded freight wagons pulled slowly away toward the south, and the two men rode back along the furrow where the small sod monuments stood like uncertain testimonials to the passing works of man. They had been put there only a year ago but already the elements had worn them down, were slowly integrating them once again with the parent sod from which they had been taken.

Back in town the Kincaid horses fretted at the hitch rail by the Lone Star Palace. Inside the place Copper Ann played at her favorite table with five men from over west, and Big Red swaggered around with his thumbs in his belt. He was a little drunk and filled with his wrongs concerning the Silver Tip which he couldn't buy. Ben Alverson was gone on the trip to Abilene.

Ann played her usual expert game and won the winter's wages from two of her opponents, but there was a change in her somehow. Her laughter was brittle, not so spontaneous, and there was less softness in her long eyes. She was still smarting under the memory of Alverson's ravishment of her lips that day on the veranda, and unconsciously she spread the blame for that indignity on all men. But she was smart enough to be her usual self, except for that new hardness in her face. For these last few days she had hated men—all men. She hated Red for his still uncertain attitude toward the stallion. She hated Velantry for that con-

temptuous refusal of her humble thanks. And there was in
her a new, unhappy bewilderment at the ways of life itself.
With the coming of the man in the good black clothes
something had gone from her world, something come into
it. Supremacy and well-being and that dead-sure Kincaid
certainty had given place to an uneasy feeling óf insecurity.

In a matter of weeks she had grown up from a reckless,
hard-riding, high-spirited girl into a woman who had begun
to think. Ann was her father's daughter, as Velantry had
said, but there was something of her mother in her, too.
Something of that gentle Jenny who had followed Big Red
to this frontier so many years ago. Jenny had been capable
of great love, great devotion, and, though no one knew it
yet, for it had had no reason to be proven, she had left
these things to her child—her only legacy. They had been
proved secondarily by Ann's devotion to Big Red, by her
fierce pride in him; but primal love, that of woman for
her man, had never touched her. She had felt its shadow in
the future, as what young girl hasn't, but its face was
featureless, its outline formless.

She had dreamed of it and waited for it and let no man
put his hands on her, and now since Ben had kissed her
and Velantry had roughly dropped her in the dust that day
she felt defiled, discredited, the spirit in her strangely
shaken.

And into the Lone Star Palace this warm afternoon
there walked a group of men whose advent was like a shock.
There was Sylvester Mead and Doak Haynes and Hilmer,
and three men from an outfit over west who were Mead's
friends. And there was Johnny Velantry. They came in
quietly, as any bunch of men might enter any public place,
with Velantry at their head, but every man in the place felt
a tingle up his spine.

Red Kincaid, lounging against the bar about halfway
down, took his heel from the rail and straightened up.

Anger flowed up across his face, and he wiped his thick lips in the thick beard with the back of his hand. He opened his mouth to roar profanely, then closed it again as his eyes met Mead's. There was something new in Sylvester's face, a quietness and indifference that had not been there in the years that he had run his store under the shadow of Big Red's tolerance—and the other saw it.

And Johnny Velantry, passing down along the bar, laid his hand on the polished edge where the passing of uncounted palms had left that lovely patina. It was the common gesture Mead had spoken of, that unrecognized desire to touch something which Copper Ann had touched, a vicarious and unconscious tribute to the girl herself. But the man in the black coat was not aware that he had made that gesture, had given that mute tribute. His black eyes were on Kincaid's angry face and they were unreadable. He waited for the other to speak, and he had not long to wait.

"What you want in here, Velantry?" Red said thinly. "You ain't to say welcome in th' Lone Star."

"It's a public saloon and gambling hall, isn't it?" Velantry asked.

"It's all of that, but I own it. I'll say who plays here or drinks here—an' I just don't like th' cut of your style."

"Or maybe you don't like the speed of my draw?"

Red looked around with shining eyes, and here and there a man rose from a table, tipped down his chair from against a farther wall. Bryce, Farloe, Spink, Harris. Sloan and Starbuck were not in town, and two other riders of the Double K stood, as usual, outside with the Fingermarks.

But Mead spoke. "This is no fighting affair, Red," he said quietly. "We just thought, with trade so slow at every place in town, we'd take a turn over here. What's wrong with that?"

"Mebbe nothin'," Kincaid said, "only we ain't open to strangers."

"We're not strangers," Velantry said. "We're business-men, like yourself, settled here."

"Mebbe you ain't so settled as you think," Big Red said mockingly.

"Oh, yes, we are. Businessmen are not so easily cleaned out as—small cattle outfits, shall we say?"

This was dynamite, and everybody knew it. The group behind Velantry knew it, but they had been primed for it in a serious hour's talk in the back room of Mead's Emporium. The three cattlemen from over west had been distant kin of the Jount boys. For years they had wished for a break with the Double K. Now they stood in a sinister silence, their faces shut and watchful.

Kincaid looked at them uneasily, a flashing glance that took them in from head to foot, and saw that they were all wearing double guns, all holstered low and tied. For the first time in many years a cold chill of premonition went down his arrogant back. He knew that all these men had been despoiled after some fashion, and all of them blamed him. All, that was, but Haynes and Hilmer—and they were here on principle. And Big Red Kincaid feared principle more than shooting irons. It always won in the end. Sometimes the far end, but in the end it won. Lightning quick, lightning hot, these things passed through his mind. And the violent dislike he had for Johnny Velantry, the whipper-snapper who had had the gall to draw on him in the open street, intensified a hundredfold that stroke of premonition. He had felt it that first day in early spring when he'd laid eyes on him. What was it? What was it in this man's dark face that always made him feel like a cat in a dark corner with strange dogs about? Who did he look like? Where had he seen that level glance, that slender, swinging grace? In the midst of this tense moment, Big Red Kincaid passed his hand across his frowning face and strove to think. And then he heard Mead speak again.

"Seems odd, Kincaid," he said, "how you keep stocked

so well. Ben's refused to do any more hauling for me or Johnny here. Wonder what's come over him?"

"Why don't you ask him?" Big Red said insolently.

"I did," Mead said. "But he didn't seem to know I was a customer of his."

"Mebbe you ain't. Mebbe you're goin' to move away, too, Ves, like this brash gambler here's goin' to. You ain't been keepin' th' right kind of company." And Big Red smiled, swaying slightly on his feet.

Velantry saw he had been drinking more than usual and was sorry. Big Red drunk, even a little drunk, did not suit his purpose. He wanted him cold sober for certain reasons. But now he caught up the opening in his words and cut in across them.

"Not all gamblers are brash," he said evenly. "I gamble but I seldom bluff—and I usually call the other man's."

"You think I'm bluffin'?" Kincaid asked. "Want to be shown?"

"Sure," Velantry answered, "that's what I came here for —to gamble. There's no one at my place to gamble with any more. Seems like you saw to that."

"I sure did, Mister," the cattleman said. "I sure as hell did."

"All right. If you don't bluff let's get down to brass tacks. I'll bet and you cover—if you've got the sand."

He pulled out a chair at a nearby table and was about to sit down when Copper Ann spoke from a little farther over, her clear young voice cleaving the silence like a blade.

"Red," she said, "let me. I can beat you any day."

"All right," her father said, "th' roof's th' limit for you, girl. And see to it you clean him to the ground."

"Done," she said briefly.

Velantry pushed back the chair he had withdrawn, stepped around it, and seated himself across from her. The others who had been playing threw in their hands as by common agreement, gathered up their winnings, and left these two alone. The girl swept the cards together, pushed them aside.

"A new pack, Curly," she called. When they came, she slid them toward Velantry. "Perhaps you'd better open them yourself," she said sarcastically.

"Perhaps I had," he said, and broke the seal.

"What will you play?" the man asked. "Straight, stud, or draw?"

"Stud," she said. "It's quicker. I think you said name bets?"

Velantry nodded.

"Then I state first," she said primly, "and I start little. I say one hundred dollars each."

Again he nodded, set the unshuffled pack between them for the cut. Ann got the deal, and her strong white hands riffled the new pasteboards beautifully. She dealt the hole card, face down, to each of them, flipped the next ones carelessly. Velantry got an eight of hearts, she a jack of spades. A queen of clubs went on the eight, a ten of spades on the jack. Each looked at the hole card.

"One hundred," Ann said.

"One hundred," he answered.

A red jack on Velantry's queen, its mate on Ann's ten.

"Another hundred," she said casually.

"Done," he said.

She threw over the last card, gave herself one. A nine of hearts for Velantry, the last jack for Ann. The girl leaned forward, folding the rest of the pack together.

"You want the say?" she said idly.

"Yes," Velantry said. "I state my say. This one hand, to be built until one or the other breaks. The great Kincaids against a—a nobody from nowhere."

He leaned back in his chair and looked up at Big Red.

There was silence at all the other tables, all over the room. The three men of the town and the three cattlemen stood close together just beyond Red, between the tables and the open doors. They could command the whole place, standing so. They would see fair play.

The girl did not even glance at her father. He had put her on her own with the roof the limit and she needed no reassurance.

"Of course," she said. "State further."

Velantry looked at her, and for the first time since he had landed in the town there was excitement in him. It was in his brilliant eyes, in the slight paleness of his face.

Within himself a die was cast. This was the beginning of the end, one way or another. Either it marked the tipping of the scales of justice which he had visioned throughout his wanderings, or it meant that he was through in this place and would be moving on.

Either way it was the beginning of the end. There was one drawback to the matter. He had not meant to use this girl in any way, nor to be used by her. He had meant to face Big Red across the final table, to beat him to the dust of loss and humiliation, not Copper Ann. Big Red he could fight with mockery and bluff and brashness. Copper Ann he must fight so, and by her own choosing.

For the long moment while these thoughts raced through his mind he sat very still, both hands on the table, his eyes, half unseeing, on her lovely face. And suddenly Ann smiled. It was her old trick, meant to distract a man, but this time it held contempt, as if she said, without words, "Scrub stock." It snapped the man erect in his chair, all regret that she was his opponent washed out of him.

"All right," he said thinly. "I state. The Silver Tip against the Lone Star Palace."

Dead silence followed the words. Astonished silence. This was that brashness of which Kincaid had accused him. And then the big man laughed.

"Hell!" he said. "Th' best saloon this side th' Llano against a has-been like th' Silver Tip?"

"Who made it so? You did. Your men have stood out

front and told all comers to stay out. Town men, trail men,
cowboys from the Llano. Your yes-man Alverson took
orders from you, too. You think to break both Mead and
me by letting no one haul for us, no one trade with us.
You've overstepped your mark this time, Kincaid. We're
not Bill Smith nor the Jount brothers. Do you bet, or are
you yellow as a snake's belly?"

For one second it seemed as if Kincaid would jump for
him. His face turned purple above the flaring beard and his
eyes shone lightning blue. His fingers crawled against his
palms, itching for a gun.

Then Ann's voice cut in above his strangled growl.
"Red," she said, "you said the roof. I'll have the Silver Tip
in just a minute. You said you'd give it to me anyway."

"Go on, girl," her father said, "it's a bet."

She looked at Velantry coldly. "I have three jacks in
sight," she said, "and a hole card. Looks like a full house
to me."

"And I," the man answered steadily, "have a possible
straight."

"You want to turn?"

"No," he said, "I am not through. I said build till one
or the other breaks. I call and you cover. Those were the
terms. If you refuse, I take without turning."

" 'Tain't fair!" Big Red yelled. "Values ain't equal!"

"They were," Velantry snapped, "before you broke the
Tip."

Ann wet her lips. "Go on," she said. "State your say."

Whatever could be said of Big Red and his methods, his
daughter was dead game. All through the years when he
had built his power and his wealth he had been thought
to be. No one had ever seen him backed into a corner, no
one had ever called a turn on him. His guns and his deadly
markmanship had backed the bluff that passed for right,
his courage had never been in question. Neither had Ann's.

Now it shone forth like a light behind her beauty. She was a little pale but she was calm. What this man meant to do to her and to her father, even to their way of life, she did not know—but he could not break that courage.

"State," she said sharply.

"I state," Velantry said into the silence, "the Bill Smith homestead which I bought"—here Big Red yelled with laughter that shook with rage—"along with all that land belonging to the Jount boys, Hez and Horace, now held by their relatives, against the Double K spread."

As if a bomb had dropped among them the nerves of every man in the place jumped and tautened. The eyes of Big Red's riders were alive in their still faces, their hands hung ready at their sides. But those six men between them and the door stood ready, too.

Kincaid licked his lips, and his wild glance took them in. He shook his head as if to clear it from the bewilderment that stunned him. For the first time in their knowledge of him he seemed to shrink a little within himself, to lose something of his stature. The Jount boys—so far back. And here stood three of their kinsmen. Bill Smith—and Elvira had called him in the open street. Something was beginning, something going wrong with the Kincaid way of life. The bullying, arrogant concept that might made right on which he had built his structure of success was breaking up beneath him. He licked his lips and flashed that lightning glance around the room again. For the first time in many years there was a coldness on the faces that looked back at him, a watchfulness, an appraisal. Only his own men seemed to offer the backing he was used to from all men. It was, somehow, as if he stood on trial, here in his own place, with his back against the bar. Sullenness and anger boiled in him and he could not speak. This Velantry— where had he seen those level brows, those temples—what did he mean to do to him? To Red Kincaid, the cattle king,

the tycoon? Why? Once more Big Red shook his head.
And then they heard Ann speak, her rich voice harsh and
brittle.

"Done," she said. "Now turn."

But Velantry did not seem to hear. He was looking at
her father. It was to him he spoke now.

"No," he said sharply, "I am not ready. I have more to
bet. Kincaid, for nearly eighteen years you've run this
country, the range, the town, the outfits. You've roared
your way to riches, by one way and another, by brag and
bluff, and you've backed your bluff with robbery and
murder."

Big Red surged forward, but Velantry's right hand lay
lightly on his coat front, and the other stopped in his
tracks. The men beside the bar, between the room full and
the open doors, were tense as cats about to spring. This
was deadly talk, shooting talk, and they expected things to
happen, but nothing did as yet. The speaker went on carefully, as if he long had planned this very scene, these words.

"Yes, robbery and murder. The Jount boys on their growing spread, prospering and young, building their herds.
They constituted a future threat to your supremacy. And
one morning there were no Jount boys, only two dead men,
riddled with bullets. And there were no Jount cattle anywhere on their range, but the Double K drove a heavy drive
to Abilene. This was long back and no one said a word to
Kincaid men, no one questioned, no matter what they
thought."

Velantry's black eyes were narrow and bright, filled with
a hard, cold fire. Bryce and Farloe, Spink and Harris behind
him stood deadly still, their gun hands sweating in the
palms, but no one made a move, for those men by the bar
were deadly still also, especially the three Jount cousins.

And Ann Kincaid was as cold and still as any there. Her
eyes on Velantry's face were wide, flaring with outraged
fury, but beginning to look beyond the man into that past

of which he spoke so insolently. It was long back and she had been a little girl, but she remembered guarded talk she'd heard around the Double K, remembered that more than ordinarily heavy drive that took all hands and was so hurried. Straining her memory she saw again her father's face in the days that followed, a wild face, filled with ready laughter, but a guarded face, too.

And she remembered the fine things he had brought back from Abilene—silk for a dress for her, red and shining, which Little Fawn had sewed clumsily into a treasured garment; the big glass pitcher and its dozen tumblers; the biggest painting in its golden frame. There had been more than ordinary opulence around the Kincaid place, a certain brittle triumph. It was long back, but she remembered. And her hands, too, were sweating now. A sickness lay inside her, something cold and heavy where her warm young heart had been, a shadow of dreadful knowledge.

She looked at Big Red's face, and for once in her life she could not read it, for things behind and beyond all her experience were written there. It looked like the face of an animal caught in a trap, before long hours of agony had dulled it, shocked and unbelieving and bewildered.

But that cold-steel voice was going on, and she forced herself to listen.

"The great Kincaid," Velantry said, his hand still on his breast, "the taker, the keeper, the bluffer! Well, you've met your match this time, old man, and I mean to see just what you're made of. I said I was not through, that I still had more to bet. I have. One of us is going out of here stripped to the skin—and I mean that literally. I take every man in this room to witness the agreement we made. I bet, you cover—or I take all stakes already set without turning up my hole card. This means all I've named so far—Lone Star, money, and the Double K. It also means my coat." With a quick shrug he shed the fine black garment. He was on his feet, and it fell on the chair behind him. "My shirt," he

said, and with his left hand he tore the buttons off in one
hard wrench, ripped it from his body, "and my undershirt."

He stood stripped to the waist, but for the soft black
holster under his left armpit, the strap across his right
shoulder, the shreds of cloth which had been beneath it.
His body shone white as a woman's, strong and thin and
muscular. His eyes on Big Red's face were terrible.

"Kincaid courage!" he said mockingly. "Or Kincaid
cowardice!"

Here Copper Ann leaped to her feet. "Match him, Red!"
she cried. "Match him! Don't let him do this to us!"

There was a wailing quality to her voice, and as her child-
ish whimper had been his law, so now it brought Big Red
straight up on his boot heels, rocked him forward on his
toes. With a roar of, "Bastard!" he grabbed his blue shirt
with the big pearl buttons down the front and pulled it
over his head. It was his only upper garment and he stood
naked to the waist himself, bronzed and bearlike, hulking
in his great size, his strength. His beard flared on his hairy
chest, his forearms were furred with hair.

And on the left side of the powerful torso, just above the
heart, there was a red, peculiar scar. A scar shaped like a
half-moon with the points turned sharply down.

At sight of it, Velantry tipped back his head and laughed.
Bitter laughter, old laughter; too old, too bitter for his
years. There was in it an ancient sorrow, and present
triumph, and the sound of future doom as sure and certain
as death itself. He flung up his left hand, snapped his fingers, and stooping, with eyes and senses still trained on
the man before him, touched that hidden hole card.

"All right," he said, "I'm ready now! Finally and completely ready! Turn your card, Miss Kin——"

He never finished the word, for in that second the whole
tense, dramatic, dangerous situation was shattered into
nothingness.

Curly Bates behind the bar had watched the scene with

perhaps the keenest appreciation in the room, the keenest anguish. The Lone Star—lost, maybe, to this hard young man from nowhere. Lost for him, Curly, in all surety, lost with all it stood for. Its activity, its excitement and—its bar. That long, lovely, shining thing with the polish of uncounted hands upon it. Hands. One hand—one pair of hands—slim, caressing hands whose touch was sacred to this humble man of glass and cloth and bottle. The hands of Copper Ann Kincaid. Never again to touch the thing that she had touched, to see her shining beauty, to feel the surge of adoration in him at her kind, impartial smile. The small eyes under the sleekly parted hair were sick with a very real distress. And Curly Bates picked up a flask half filled with liquor which gave it weight, hefted it in his hand. He wrapped it quickly in one of his clean white cloths, swung it lightly to get its balance, and let drive with it straight across the bar. It struck the surface of that table between the man and girl and swept it clean. Layouts and pack, the cards that held the fate of Curly and the Lone Star Palace, to say nothing of the rest, lay in a hopeless jumble on the sanded floor. No one now could know, would ever know, what had topped those jacks in Ann's layout, whether or not Velantry had had the straight which would have beaten her.

For a moment no one moved. Then the girl drew a long, hard breath and looked up at Red Kincaid. She did not speak, but Big Red threw back his head and this time it was his laughter, bull-throated, triumphant, half-hysterical, which filled the place. He stuck his thumbs in his belt and rolled drunkenly on his feet.

"Beat down th' Kincaids?" he yelled, shouting. "Or Kincaid people? Hell's bells! It can't be done! Ain't meant to be!"

Without a word Velantry picked up his coat and hat and, carrying them in his left hand, walked past the girl without a glance at her. He joined the six men by the bar and all of them, some walking backward, left the place in a compact group.

They tramped across the street and a little way down to Mead's Emporium where they halted on the porch. Velantry wiped his forehead with the palm of his hand, and he was shaking visibly. They watched him gravely and all had a troubled feeling that here was more, much more, than was apparent on the surface.

"Balked," he said bitterly, "because a damn bartender threw a bottle! If that had gone through we'd have run Kincaid out of the country—by force if he'd tried to hedge. We were all witnesses to the given and accepted bets."

"I wish it had gone through," Hiram Jount said quietly. "Them cousins of mine was good boys. Hez had seven bullets in him. Well, mebbe there'll be another time."

"Maybe there will, Hiram," Velantry said, "and I thank you for being with us. Your presence did something to Kincaid. I could see it in his face."

"Johnny," Sylvester Mead said curiously, "I'm wondering just what that hole card was. Whether or not you had that flush, or if you was just bluffing. I ain't asking, I'm just wondering."

"A bluff's a serious thing, Ves," Johnny said soberly. "Many a man's died with his boots on because of one. On the other hand, that was a good layout to fill."

Chapter Eleven

AFTER THAT DAY IN THE LONE STAR PALACE JOHNNY VELAN-try became a harder man than he had been before. There was no lightness in him, no laughter.

He kept more to himself, spent longer hours away from the Silver Tip on those seemingly aimless rides across the rolling prairies, and the long dark thoughts intensified within him. And there was something else inside him, too, something which filled him with new bitterness. This was the memory of Ann Kincaid's blue eyes turned up to his that breathless moment when he had held her against his breast and ridden out the Ringer's flashing speed. Memory of her parted lips so near his own, her humble words. And memory of his bitter harshness when he half dropped her in the dusty road. Why did it have to be that this girl was mixed up in the tragic thing which he must do? Why did Big Red have to be her father? And why did a woman's hand bear down upon his heart so heavily now? He who had forsworn all women more than three lonely years ago? His clenched fist struck down upon his saddle horn at that, his mouth was set and hard. His goal was set, his die was cast, and all the meaning of his life was in them.

He meant to kill Big Red Kincaid, but he meant to ruin him first, to sweep away his treasured things, to clean him to the ground—as Kincaid had cleaned another man nearly twenty years ago. A young man, an honorable man, who had turned old before his time and who had died dishonored. A man who, innocent, now filled a felon's grave and who had left behind him the heritage of a tarnished name. . . . Thinking so, Velantry would remove his hat and let the summer winds cool his sweating temples.

121

Things were changing in the town, slowly, almost imper-
ceptibly, but changing. Men from the ranges began once
more to come to gamble at the Silver Tip, careful-eyed,
careful-spoken men who knew things which they could
not prove. No one could actually prove who killed the
Jount boys or who had sold their branded stock. Double K
riders still lounged along the rail in front registering with
their eyes all those who went into the place; but where, a
month before, many a foot would have hesitated, perhaps
turned back, their owners now trod grimly up the wide
board steps.

A month ago they would have feared reprisal, sly, un-
provable, but not to be mistaken. Perhaps a few hundred
head of scattered longhorns run off their ranges, perhaps
a priceless water hole found dynamited. Now they felt a
new thing in the country, saw small straws in the wind.
They had seen the Kincaid outfit matched and almost
beaten, for every man jack in the Lone Star that dramatic
day believed that Johnny Velantry had not been bluffing.
They believed he had had the Kincaids whipped, that only
Kincaid treachery in the form of Curly Bates had saved
them from the greatest cleaning the rangeland had ever
seen. They knew a showdown had been slated, that it still
was slated, if this Velantry lived to pull it off—and after
the fashion of the pack, either wolf or man, they began to
draw in behind what might prove to be a young, new
leader. Not that the world of the cattle country had ever
followed Red. It had laid off him, merely. No one had ever
called him, none openly opposed him or the men who
formed his outfit. No one had dared.

Ben Alverson came back from Abilene, but he got no
time alone with Copper Ann. The girl was changing, too.
She came less often to the town, the joy of life seemed
dulled in her. When she rode Stormwind down the one
street it was with a hard hand on his rein, a sterner mastery

than she had displayed toward him before. The stallion seemed to sense this, too, and fretted at the restraint, tossing his handsome head, shaking the foretop from his eyes, pounding the earth with his iron-shod feet.

She met Alverson on the porch of her father's store where she had gone with the list of household supplies, her habit skirt looped at her knee, her bright head bare as usual, and the man looked at her so deeply that she flushed in spite of herself. That flush raced the blood in his usually quiet veins, for it seemed to tell him something. That she felt his presence, recalled that kiss. But her face was graver than he had ever seen it; her eyes avoided his.

Don't know her own heart yet, he told himself. "Hello, Ann," he said aloud.

"Hello, Ben," she answered soberly, and passed him without more words.

The man looked after her anxiously, but, with that artistry inherent in him, let her go. Time enough. He'd go out to the ranch again soon.

But before that time came he'd heard about the game in the Lone Star Palace, and a rage as deep as Big Red's own flared up in him against Velantry. Driven by his feeling about this girl, anything which touched her touched him. An enemy of her father or herself was his enemy also. So the dark clouds thickened about Velantry's head.

Ann Kincaid was driven, too. Those dark memories of the past stood like a moving curtain against which all her life, and Big Red's, passed like a play. A deep play, sinister, frightening in its implications, little understood.

"You knew my mother, Fawn," she said to the Indian woman. "Was she a happy woman? Did she love my father?"

Little Fawn glanced at her with unusual quickness. "Good woman," she said softly, her opaque eyes turned

back across the years. "She good woman. Love ever'thing.
Puppies. Kittens. People. Sweet, like early mornin'."

"No. That's not an answer," Ann said doggedly. "Was
she happy?"

"Course she was."

"Always? At the last? Not just at first when they came
here?"

Little Fawn sprinkled furiously at the garments she was
damping down to iron. "What you get at?" she asked
sharply. "Why you ask these?"

"Because I want to know," Ann said, "to understand a
lot of things."

This brown woman, quiet, hard-working, faithful, had
been a wall around the girl since babyhood, a sword and a
buckler in a world of men, and she had never lied to her.
Evasive, yes, if it was needful, clam-silent too at times, but
Ann had never doubted her, had never found a flaw in her
uprightness. Now she watched her, waiting. And Little
Fawn looked down upon her work with those back-seeing
eyes. And presently she drew a deep breath like a sigh and
answered.

"Mebbe not ever-ever," she said. "Mebbe not last. Little
'fore last."

"How long before last?"

"Little. Mebbe summer, mebbe spring. She cry an' cry,
them times."

The girl felt a stab of pain for that mother whom she
hardly knew, hardly remembered. The young and pretty
thing brought here from half across a world, from all she'd
ever known, following Big Red because she loved him.
And Red had loved her, that Ann knew beyond all doubt.
But what had happened at that last? What dreams had
dimmed and darkened? What idols had lain shattered?
And when? Was it about the time, so far away, when the
Jount boys had died? No, for Ann remembered that, the

talk, the furtive hilarity. So it must have been before. Early in the days of the Double K, when Big Red was coming up to the slowly mounting affluence that marked his later life. Was it something Jenny'd learned about his methods, the driving might that made up his conception of right?

"How come?" she asked the woman now. But Fawn had said all she meant to say. She gathered up her basket of damped-down clothes and waddled off, and Ann frowned, thinking.

So another woman had loved Big Red as she had, with idolatry, had been disillusioned as she was being disillusioned. Jenny and Ann. Both upright and honest, loving the things of right and justice, and both casting the pearls of their devotion before the swine of arrogance and wrong and cruelty.

The world, the good green world of rolling plain and gentle, willowed stream, had changed within these last few months, its wild joy calmed, its sunlight darkened. Changed with the coming of a man—one man, young and handsome, in a fine black coat, whose very touch had blighted it. The cold, hard hatred which had burned in her against this man was changing, too. Changing into fear. Why did Velantry cling upon her father's trail relentlessly? What did he know? What was he trying to find out? Why did he mean to break the richest man in all the country? To drag the proud tycoon in the dust? Why? Why? She could not find an answer, but that there was one she felt deep in her inmost heart.

Big Red felt it, too. Beneath all his bewilderment and rage and sullen resentment he sensed the presence of a deeper thing than was apparent on the surface of this man's enmity, but what it was he could not figure out. There had been much in his own life to warrant vengeance, but it was covered. Safely, finally, and forever covered, he was as sure as that he lived. Which of his misdeeds was catching up

with him he could not know. He could, however, know the
change that was occurring in himself. The inroads of unease and nervousness and fear. Yes, fear! In him, who had
not known the face of fear for nearly half a lifetime! The
arrogance, the pride, the unbeatable strength which had
been the foundation of his climb to wealth and power
were breaking up. The institution that had been Big Red
Kincaid was shaking—and only Big Red knew it! Knew it
with a baffled fury, since he did not know how or why. He
was like a wounded bull, hurt and rumbling, raising his
crested shoulders for the fight. As Velantry meant to finish
him, coldly and with calculated plan, so he rallied his vast
courage and his half-animal cunning to the same end, but
with a difference. He was mad and hot and dangerous, hair-
trigger hung, ready to explode upon a touch.

Between two days, Velantry left the town. He went by
the Smith homestead, talked in the starlight with Sam
Bolin, left him a few provisions, and vanished into the
illimitable distances to the south-by-southwest. He rode for
a few hours and was swallowed up in the beautiful, un-
peopled stretches of the Llano Estacado. He let the Ringer
take his little running walk which seemed so trifling slow
but which covered such an amazing amount of ground,
slept for an hour by a nameless stream, and with the dawn
was moving on again. For one day, two, he went his lonely
way, subsisting sparingly on the dried meat, the hardtack,
in the small roll behind his saddle. The Ringer fared much
better on the tall bunch grass which clothed the world as
far as eye could see. Here there were cattle, longhorned,
branded, belonging to those far-scattered outfits whose
owners and riders played sometimes at the Silver Tip, but
Johnny Velantry kept to the lower dips and long rolling
hollows, avoiding this and that home ranch whose buildings were visible from time to time.

On the morning of the third day he drew down along a little creek and came upon a small spike camp; a cabin, a barn and several sizable corrals. He stopped well out in the open, halloed, and sat with his hands crossed on the saddle bow.

As if a spring had popped him out a man with a rifle appeared in the doorway, stepped out in the yard. He was the typical spike-camp tender, a worn-out cowboy, too old for active duty, in charge of the lonely place, a day's ride from its nearest neighbor, ready to cook for any and all riders who might come that way, answering to some outfit but chary of names. He was lean and brown, with the bandy legs of long association with horse and saddle, sandy mustaches, and the veiled and hooded eyes of secrecy. He did not speak.

Velantry named himself, and Frank and Seastron Daunce. At that, as if the names were magic, what passed for a cordial smile twitched the scraggly whiskers.

"Glad to see ye, Mr. Velantry," the man said gracefully. "Light down an' eat. I got a pot of right fresh beans a-cookin'. On'y ben on sence day before yestiddy."

So Velantry dismounted, unsaddled and turned the, Ringer into the first corral where there was hay in the open barn, washed at the bench behind the cabin, and presently sat down to the coarse and nourishing food of the far places, steak and biscuit, beans and coffee. He knew the spoonbread of the South, its juleps and fried chicken, had eaten prawns at New Orleans and enchiladas at Juarez, but of them all this common fare was best, as of the time and place and condition of his appetite.

Not until he was fully satisfied did the business of this long and lonely ride take place. As by common consent both men rose from the clean pine table, lighted the cigars which Johnny produced, and stepped out in the open yard. Not for nothing had Velantry pulled his dragnet along all the edges of this far frontier. He knew better than to mention private things except in the clear, away from walls, even in such lonely solitude as this.

They smoked for a little while in the comfortable silence that obtains after food. Then Velantry spoke, low-voiced and careful.

"How long," he asked, "before you'll be seeing Frank and Stron?"

" 'Bout a week, I cal'late," the other said. "They'll be by here on th' way up north."

"Be driving?" Still on that cautious tone. It seemed to satisfy the other.

"Yup," he said. "Sizable trail-herd. In from over west, under th' Capitans."

"Bound for Abilene?"

"You oughta know," the other answered, "if you know Frank an' Stron."

"I know them. Frank gave you my name, didn't he? My description? Told you what I'd be likely to say?"

"Yes, sir, he did. An' you'll excuse me, Mr. Velantry, but a man's got to be cautious. Got to look after his boss' interests, I'd say."

"I know. All right. Now listen. When the boys come by here you tell Frank I was here today, and that I said, 'The time is ripe.' Just that."

"That all?"

"That's all. But don't forget. And tell him by himself. Be sure of that. Tell him in private."

"I won't forget," the camp tender said.

"Thanks for the meal. Those were the best beans, bar none, I ever ate," Velantry said, smiling. "And now I'll be starting back. You might like these," and he took the last of the cigars from his vest pocket and gave them to him.

Without more words he went to the corral, saddled Ringer, gave him water, mounted, waved his hand, and rode away, back trail toward the north and east. The thing he had come so far to do was done; another wheel in the machinery of Red Kincaid's undoing was set in motion.

It was sundown two days later when Velantry came home to the Silver Tip. The Ringer was gaunt but very fit, and so was the man who rode him. No one knew where they had been; none asked. Not even Sylvester Mead looked a question. Only the women whispered in the town's backyards.

"He's mysterious, if you ask me," one said.

"Maybe. But it looks as if Ann likes that kind."

"Ha! She hates the ground he walks on since he pulled her off of Stormwind's back that day!"

"You're wrong," the quiet one put in. "You don't know women. It's the perfect setup to attract her to him."

But only this one person seemed to know that ancient fact. Even Copper Ann herself did not know it; she, too, thought she hated John Velantry. Big Red was sure she did. Ben Alverson was thoughtful in the matter. And he was not sure he had been right that day on the veranda, now when she looked everywhere but in his eyes. She was the Untouchable and he had overstepped that lifelong barrier. He would have given his right hand to be able to recall that kiss.

Big Red Kincaid flaunted himself about the town, swaggering, half drunk at times, filled with riotous laughter. It was as if he bolstered up some inner weakness with an outer seeming of untrammeled strength.

Word of the situation at the settlement reached far and wide across the ranges. More and more men came into town to drink and gamble and to see what might develop any day or night or hour. But though the place was strung like a taut wire, nothing happened. Velantry kept to the Silver Tip, and though the Double K riders still lounged around outside, Big Red himself did not come near. And for the first time since she had learned to play two years

before, Copper Ann no longer graced her father's tables.
The tang was gone from winning; life had somehow lost its
savor. Only the lonely reaches of the prairies, the racing
power of the stallion's speed, the strong wind of his going
in her face, gave her their old comfort, their old and heady
grace.

Chapter Twelve

CHAD SHALLY'S TEAMS CAME CREEPING UP THE TRAIL. THEY stopped one noon at the plowed furrow, received instructions from the two men who waited there, and pulled slowly on toward Abilene, lost in their own dust.

And deep in the Llano Estacado the Daunce boys drifted into the lone spike camp by the nameless stream behind a big trail-herd. Bawling, wild-eyed, their rumps half-healed where running iron and new brand had overlaid old markings, the cattle crawled across the plains to north and east, toward Abilene and railhead where so many of their kind had disappeared.

A more than ordinarily large remuda followed them; they were fringed with riders, many riders. These were hard men, as hard as the mild, soft-spoken Daunces, gathered from the illimitable spaces of the Staked Plains, reckless, spoiling for excitement. That that excitement was likely to arise from gun smoke in the night, from outlaw pitted against cattleman, they knew full well and welcomed. It was the only kind they knew.

And so the stage of open range and little town, of right and wrong, of vengeance and the belated evening of an ancient score, was set and waiting, but only John Velantry knew it to be so. There was a tenseness in him these days, a great stillness in his long, fine hands. He was readying himself for what might well be the final act of his life. What he, one man alone, had undertaken to do was no small thing. Rather it savored of the fantastic, the impossible, for it was the destruction, financially, spiritually, and physically, of the most powerful man in the country. And no one knew better than he, with his long training in the

131

appraisal of men, how powerful, how bullheadedly courageous that man was.

Pig Red Kincaid had despoiled others, whooping with laughter. When his turn came, as it certainly must, it would be another matter; and he would not stop at death itself. Whether his death or Velantry's, who could say?

But either way Velantry was ready. Fully ready now. Often at night, in the bleak back room behind the Silver Tip, he would take from the pocket of the coat the mysterious packet that never left his possession, spread its contents on the table, and study them with somber eyes. He knew ,by heart each word, each line, each article. Old words, old articles, worn by his years on trail and saddle and sacred to him as nothing in the world was sacred. Meager contents, consisting only of three things, a crease-worn letter and two photographs, which held the tragedy of his life. The letter made this concrete, but it was not needed in the light of the two faces pictured there. Some years back when Velantry was a younger man he had wept in secret at the sight of them, the bitter tears of youth, the tears of love and loss and undying shame. The face of a woman, young and lovely, with eyes as black as Velantry's own, with his wavy, jet-black hair, a laughing, loving, happy face. And the face of a slim blond man whose brows were winged and straight before his handsome temples, the veritable brows which, but for their coloring, bent down above them now in the light from a coal-oil lamp.

Color of one, form of the other, this somber man was of them both.

Taken some several years apart, the pictured faces told a stark story. The woman's, joy and pride and well-being. The man's—in a striped coat with a number on his breast— despair; final, hopeless, deep as hell itself. Long Velantry would look at them these summer nights, silent, sad, hard with a hardness beyond his years, his face pinched about the lips with the renewal of old vows. Then he would gather up these shabby things and put them back in the leather packet with hands as gentle as a woman's.

And in the week that followed two things were afoot in the rangeland. The Daunce boys, after receiving the message waiting for them at the spike camp, swung their trail-herd sharply north to parallel the Chisholm Trail far over west and to by-pass the cattle town; and the first of the final showdowns between Velantry and Big Red Kincaid took place in the open street.

This happened suddenly as things of vital import so often do. It was a Saturday and horses, buckboards, wagons lined the hitch rails before saloon and store. Stockmen and riders, in town to drink and gamble, to see what might be stirring; women in calico and gingham dresses doing their trading at the two big stores—they made a pleasant bustle in the slow, warm day. It was significant that Mead's Emporium did as brisk a business as ever, despite the Kincaid efforts. The straws in the wind of what had been happening since the early spring, when the stranger in the black coat had ridden in from nowhere, had begun to tell their tale, to have an effect. Folk did not walk so softly before the Kincaid outfit, were not so quick to step aside when the boss of the Double K came tearing down the street on Streaker, his blue eyes darting with lights of laughter in them, the great beard flaring on his breast.

And so he came this day, arrogant again, filled with his old vanity, the uncertainties, the shameful weaknesses in him gendered by Velantry's presence and his enmity, swept aside by the harsh, courageous spirit in him which needed only a little time to rebuild itself. Sulking at home for days on end he had convinced himself once more of Kincaid invincibility, of Kincaid might which made the only right he'd ever known.

So now he rode in laughing, his red head bare; and he looked like some ancient Viking god on the back of the great pink mare with her cloud of creamy mane, her wild blue eyes. Streaker was a fit mount for any god—monstrous, pounding, swift, arrogant as the man she carried. Behind them rode Sloan and Farloe, Spink and Bryce and Fisher.

Johnny Velantry, headed for Mead's Emporium, was halfway across the street when Big Red bore down upon him. It looked as if the rider meant to trample the man before him, and perhaps he did. Folk on the porches of the two stores, the saloons, stopped in their tracks, arrested by the imminence of action whose outcome none might foresee.

And square in the middle of the road John Velantry stopped, too. His cold eyes fixed on the thundering apparition, he stood like a rock and his right hand was stiffly spread, the fingers flexing slightly at the tips. Every gunman within sight saw and knew the motion, the deadly motion of the expert shot. Big Red saw it too and drew the roan mare sharply up so that her sliding forefeet left long ribbons in the dust.

"Get out of my way!" he yelled.

But Velantry did not move. Instead he raised his left hand slowly and pushed the wide hat back from his forehead so that all might see his face—a grave face, suddenly tensed.

"Who says I must?" he asked clearly.

"I do, you damned whippersnapper!"

"And who are you?" the younger man said distinctly.

"Ah-h-h-h!" It was a snarling sound, filled with a huge disgust.

"Ah, yes!" Velantry said. "Kincaid, I believe. Big Red Kincaid. The cattle king, the tycoon. The richest man north of the Llano. When Big Red speaks the populace trembles."

"Will you get out of my way an' let a man ride by?" Red shouted furiously.

"I will not," Velantry said, still in that clear, carrying voice. It was as if he wanted this large and intently silent audience to hear his words, to get a picture of the situation which could not afterward be blurred. That oddly spread right hand lay just across the middle of his lean young stomach. Somewhere a woman drew a long breath like a sigh.

"He's all alone!" she said distinctly. "There's no one with him!"

Velantry did not take his eyes from Big Red's face, but he answered her politely.

"Thank you, lady," he said, "but no, ma'am, I'm not alone. There are two people, both long dead, right here beside me. Two people, one of whom Big Red should remember, whom he could not possibly forget. I speak for him—for that man who, dead though he is, still lives profoundly."

Velantry's eyes were blazing now with a light to match Red's own.

"Kincaid," he said mockingly. "Mister Kincaid—or should I say Concannon? Martin P. Concannon, from a small town in Missouri, who once knew a man by the name of Holt. William Henry Holt. Do you remember him, Kincaid?"

If the cattlemen and their families, gathered in the town for the weekly trading, had looked for drama they saw it now. They saw the man on the red roan mare slump sidewise in his saddle, clutching for its horn. They saw the face under the swept-back, flaming hair turn deathly white, shining like a moon in fog. They saw the mouth in the red beard open wide for the breath that had seemingly been squeezed out of his lungs. The saw Big Red collapse inwardly upon himself. Saw Ennis Sloan kick the barren stud Sunbolt forward to Streaker's side, saw him reach out and pull Kincaid upright again. They did not hear the sighing whisper that was Big Red's voice.

"Th' temples!" the tycoon breathed. "Th' dam' temples and eyebrows! Black, not blond! I might have known!"

Over beyond the barber shop Stella Adams stood self-effacingly among the dusty weeds that fringed the path, and her big white fingers crawled in her palms at the look of Big Red's face, the slumping of his great body. Pain like that of death stabbed through her.

"Oh, my dear!" she cried inwardly. "What have they done to you?"

But Velantry was through for the time being. He had called Kincaid and seen him crumble. All the silent crowd had seen him crumble. He had scored his first showdown. So he flung up his hand and snapped his fingers and moved on across the dust toward Mead's Emporium, but his eyes turned back toward the Kincaid men, watchful, ready, expecting anything.

But the Double K was done, too, for the time. Turning like automatons these body-and-soul-bought riders crowded in around Big Red, and with the foreman's arm still around him, they went slowly out of town.

People breathed again; low voices murmured.

And Johnny Velantry went into the Emporium and looked at Sylvester, asked for some unimportant thing he'd come to buy, paid for it, and tramped back across the street to his own place.

Stella Adams, forgetting what her errand was at the store, walked back across the little bridge in the willows with unseeing eyes. She would have given her right hand to have had Big Red brought to the hiding comfort of her cabin, but she could not disgrace him so, in broad daylight, before the condemning eyes of the people. Whatever else this woman was, there lived in her a love beyond all selfish gain, a devotion worthy of a better cause.

And there had been born in her that hour a hatred of the black-clad man who shamed the tycoon before those who had feared him. She could have killed Velantry with a good grace.

It was early dusk when Big Red with his men behind him

came into the home ranch at the Double K, and Ann swung idly in the keg-stave hammock.

With the first sight of them she stopped swinging, sat up. As Red stepped off of Streaker he swayed drunkenly, but she knew he was not drunk. She came to her feet, watching in silence. Watched him come up the path like one gone suddenly ill and went to meet him, her hand on his arm.

"What is it, Red?" she asked anxiously, but her father did not answer, and over his shoulder Ennis Sloan looked at her with guarded, eloquent eyes.

"He's had a little turn," he told her quietly. "Be all right come morning."

But he was wrong. Kincaid went straight to his own room and to his bed. Little Fawn, taking him some supper, came out with the full plate and closed the door.

"What is?" Ann asked her fearfully, and the woman shook her head. Like Sloan, she said comfortably, "No hungry. All right tomorrow." But she knew she lied to comfort the girl.

And in the morning Big Red was not all right. He was never to be all right, truly all right, as long as he lived. Never again to be the roaring, arrogant bully, the thief, the killer. The unease, the strange spiritual weakness which had been growing in him all through the spring and early summer, had snapped into a shaking, deadly fear with those few words spoken by a young man in the open street. Words from a past he had long thought dead and buried, never to see the light of day again.

But here it was, that past, standing naked in the town in the form of a strange man out of nowhere, a gambler, a fly-by-night, who looked at him with knowing eyes and taunted him with mockery. His big hands shook so that he could hardly feed himself; his face was still the color of raw dough above his flaming beard.

And the heart of his daughter yearned toward him. No

matter what changes had taken place in her thought of him, what fears and dreads and disillusionments had come to dwell with her, vaguely but persistently, she was still his daughter, and she had loved him above all other things.

Loved his strength, his surety, his success. Best of all she had loved the roistering, laughing, hard-riding spirit in him that brooked defeat in nothing, rode the top wave always. And now she saw that spirit broken, the arrogance departed. Watching him at that breakfast table she could have cried with pity. Pity for the shifting eyes, the bloodless skin, the shaking hands. And she, too, could have killed Velantry, though with a difference. Where Stella Adams hated him completely, Copper Ann hated him with reservations. The reservations of sober acknowledgment of reasons, the recognition of some drive behind Velantry and directed against her father which stemmed from something which she did not know, but which she thought Big Red did know.

And so the slow days passed—two, three, a week—and Kincaid did not leave the home ranch. Twice Ann went into town to order from the store, but it was Sloan who accompanied her, Spink and Starbuck who followed with the wagon, and she did not go near the Lone Star Palace. Passing, she raised her eyes, somber now, no longer gay with laughter, to its familiar open doors and wished it was that carefree early spring again.

On one of these trips she saw Velantry in the street and, to save her life, she could not help but look at him deeply, resentment on her troubled face. And the man looked back as deeply. What was it between these two, pitted against each other across a gulf of some mysterious wrong, that drew them toward each other as with an unseen cord? The innocent young girl did not know. Velantry knew too well. And on this day he wished profoundly that he had never struck this little frontier town, had never followed here the trailwise talk of a monstrous red-haired man who ruled his lonely world. His mouth shut grimly at the thought, for this was heresy and treason. Treason to the pictured faces in the precious wallet, to the whole aim and dedication of his life.

Ann saw Ben Alverson that day, too, though Alverson had seen her first, had witnessed that odd, strange look she gave Velantry, and felt his heart contract. He came to her across the dusty road and smiled down at her, his handsome, heavy face gentle as only the sight of her could gentle it. The gray wings on his temples stood out strikingly in the sunlight when he took off his hat.

"Hello, Ann," he said softly. "How's Big Red?"

"Not so good," she answered straightly. "I'm worried about him."

"I'd like to see him. Be all right if I come out? Say tomorrow night?"

"Surely. You're always welcome at the Double K, Ben. You know that. And Red is fond of you. Do him good, maybe."

"All right. Be out a little before sundown. I hope I'm welcome with you too, Ann," he added, half pathetically. Ann forced her eyes to meet his squarely.

"Of course you are," she said honestly. "You always have been, always will be."

She saw his weathered face light up, and all her after life she would be glad she'd said those kindly words that seemed to voice a promise.

She passed Stella Adams on the store porch, and with the fierce contempt of all good woman of her time for those of Stella's stamp, she gave her a wide berth, raised her head, averted her eyes.

Two women, trading at the counter, smiled secretly at each other. "What she don't know!" one whispered.

"I'm glad she don't," the other murmured kindly. "She's a sweet, good girl, and that knowledge could just about destroy her."

And Stella Adams, going along the path with her small purchases in her arms, sighed heavily. It was the veritable breath of sorrow, a living, ever-present regret for the little honest house that had never been, for a big man tramping openly in at mealtime and at night, not furtively with the shadows, and—who knew?—maybe for a tall and slender daughter with the big man's shining hair. Truly this woman, who had recognized too late her vast capactity for love, was paying dearly for the hoard of gold in the container on the shelf.

Over west of town a matter of four or five miles, the crawling dust-gray blanket of a large trail-herd slowly ate its way toward the north. Its remuda, so large that no horse in it was worked down, rambled lazily behind; its many riders were fiddle-fit and slowly building with that odd, unholy excitement shot with deadly peril which presaged a raid; its two bosses, Frank and Seastron Daunce, were tight-lipped, bright of eye, thinking of Abilene and the markets there. Secret markets among the honest ones, which took all brands, straight, altered, or frankly ironed, and asked no questions. Took horses, too, at stiff prices, if they were good.

Grinning to himself, Frank Daunce wondered what such horses as he had seen some months ago, at a hitch rail in a little town, horses like a dream of immortal studs, with blue eyes in their ivory and silver faces and the sharp, distinguishing marks of tarry fingers at their slender knees, would bring.

A fortune, that was what. A veritable fortune for such men as he and Stron.

Chapter Thirteen

SO ALL THE THREADS OF THIS SMALL DRAMA OF THE LONELY
land were drawing in toward the end, to that final fling of
wrong and vengeance, of love and hate and blazing action
which was to set its mark forever on the place, to affect
so many lives.

Some of those many riders from the trail-herd went
ahead to scout the plains, returned to talk with Frank
Daunce at the night campfires.

"Range is lousy with cattle," they told him. "Good
stock, fat, big. Pretty well scattered. Throwed in around
some water holes up north, a lot about middle between
there an' Bent Bow Creek which runs right through th'
Double K, down to th' home place an' beyond. Bunch of
right hard-lookin' riders, 'bout nine should say. All go
armed, of course. Big boss, redheaded, don't look too fitten.
Got a redheaded girl. Saw her out by herself, ridin' th' most
wonderful stallion I ever laid eyes on. I'd druther have her
than all them amazin' horses."

"Lay off," Frank Daunce said sharply. "You touch her
an' we'll have every man on this range ridin' hell-bent after
us. Her father, th' stock, th' men, they'll be a handful—
but th' girl's another matter, an' I want no part of her.
They call her Copper Ann an' say no man's ever touched
her, personal. So lay off her, strictly, all of you, or I'll make
you wish you had."

The night was fairly dark, but the great stars of the
open country blazed beautifully in the heavens. Daunce
gave orders to bed the trail-herd early that the cattle might
rest the fore part of the night, for they would be traveling
later and very fast. So the riders caught up fresh mounts

from the loose remuda and began to circle the great gray
blanket close at its edges. Evenly spaced and heading in
the same direction, these men of the prairies began their
age-old ritual of calm and quiet. Walking their horses,
smoking their silky, cornhusk, Mexican cigarettes, they took
up, one by one, the singing which the first man out had
started. Tenor, bass, and baritone, they made a lovely music
in the silent dark—high, clear, plaintive. They sang the
songs of trail and camp and cow town, with long-drawn
nuances of love and loss and heartbreak so dear to men of
their time and place and occupation, and it was a known
fact that many a life had been saved by the music, many a
stampede averted. The cattle, poor dumb brutes bound for
the tragedy of cattle chute and rattling train and eastern
stockyard, seemed to fall beneath its spell, to trust the men
who made it.

And presently the longhorns, sidling in together as the
riding circle narowed, knelt by the forepart, sank down by
the hind, drew windy breaths of comfort, and fell to chew-
ing the sweet cuds they had gathered in the day. After a
while that, too, would cease for the time and they would
sleep.

A few miles over east the peace of the summer twilight
lay over the home ranch at the Double K. Big Red sat in his
favorite chair on the wide veranda, and swung slowly in the
hammock, the boys sat or lay around on the beaten earth
beyond, and Ben Alverson sat tilted back against the wall.
He had driven out again with the light buckboard, hoping
to get the girl to drive with him, but no opportunity had
offered. Silent, his thoughts heavy in his mind, he watched
her in the shadows, the smoke from his cigar making lazy
clouds about his head.

They talked, as men will everywhere in the summer dusk,
of times, cows, water, the price of beef—all the things that
go to make life and its interests. But it was Sloan who took

the lead for the outfit now, since Big Red was so silent. Ann was silent, too, and the conversation presently languished and only the cigarettes, glowing like fireflies in the peaceful night, spoke of the humans behind them.

The Fingermarks, those lovely creatures of fire and grace and unclocked speed, padded restlessly in the dust of Big Corral, blew and whistled in the dark.

In the kitchen, lighted by a coal-oil lamp hung before its tin reflector on the wall, Little Fawn sang some wordless melody, primitive as her people and herself. The stars of early night swung slowly down the blue vault of the sky and, for some vague, unrealized reason, these folk, who were usually abed with darkness, sat on in the quiet evening. Perhaps it was because of that strange undertone of sadness which was everpresent now at the Double K; or was it something yet more vague, a premonition, maybe, a sense of unrest beneath the restfulness?

The cigarettes were finished, ground out in the warm dust, fresh ones rolled and lighted, and still no one made a move to rise. Ben Alverson thought of the girl so close beside him, yet so far away in her aloofness, and the memory of that ravished kiss poured hot along his veins. She was thinking, too, but it was not of him. She saw Velantry's face, and took her mind away from that vision, and returned to it again. She, too, felt a fire in her blood and did not know its name. She called it hatred and contempt and like unhappy things, but it was there, to fade and die away and flash back like a light seen through the troubled darkness of a storm.

But the thoughts of Big Red Kincaid were the darkest, most painful of them all. None knew them but himself—perhaps one other!—nor would ever know them, for they dealt with a dead past come to life, with the payment for that past which he knew was in the making, now, this very day, this very hour. How literally true that was, however, he could not know just then. He was to know it soon

—before that big bright star had touched the tops of the tall cottonwoods over west where the Bent Bow made a graceful bend.

Before it was quite down Ben Alverson let down the front legs of his chair, reached for the hat beside him on the earthen floor.

"Well," he said, "I guess I'll be getting on back to town. The wagons roll for Abilene a little early in the morning. See you later, folks."

"Come again, Ben," Big Red said heavily. "Always like to see you."

"Sure I will, Red," the tall man answered. Then he held out his hand to Ann who had risen and stood quietly beside him, a slender figure, lance- straight, lance-proud. He always thought of her so. What a girl she was! What a woman for a man to have beside him—if she loved him. He drew a deep breath, patted her slim hand.

"So long, Ann," he said. "Stormwind seems on th' rampage tonight. That highest whistle his?"

"Yes," she said. "He's been high all week. Must ride him out tomorrow. Rest are fretsome, too. They don't get enough work to——"

She never finished what she had meant to say, for two men got swiftly to their feet in the open yard; Ennis Sloan rose like a cat on his boot heels. They stood so, strung like suddenly taut wire, listening with the keen hearing of men who live in the open.

What those three heard was so faint, so far away, as to be inaudible to the others, but it was there, a dim, thin thread of sound, sustained, too highly pitched. It came downwind from over at the west and north, out of that stretch of rolling prairie where the Jount boys had run their promising herds so long ago, and it was the bawling of cattle, many cattle, massed and moving. It was not yet stampede, these men of the sharp ears knew, but it could soon be so. There was in it the rising wail of coming hysteria which could send six thousand head of longhorns flowing like a tide of madness across the fenceless levels.

Without a word Sloan started for the corrals, every man jack on the brand coming fast behind him. Big Red rose uncertainly, staring after them.

"Boys!" he cried. "What th' hell? What's up?"

"Maybe nothin'," Sloan called back. "Maybe a run. Sounds like th' stock's movin' over northwest. We better go see."

"Saddle Streaker. I'll go too."

Ann turned to him, anxiety on her face. "No, Red," she said, "don't go. It's a dark night and Streaker's pretty high. Let the boys go."

"Out of my way, girl," Kincaid said harshly. "What you tryin' to do? Lay me on th' shelf? Well, I ain't to say dodderin' yet. Where my riders go, I go, an' don't forget it."

He strode away after the men, and Alverson stood a moment thinking. Then he touched the girl's arm gently. "Don't fret," he said. "I'll just go along, to see the old boy keeps out of trouble."

"Thanks, Ben," Ann said gratefully. "He's not been himself for days on end. I think he's failing. I'll be glad to have you ride with him. Take Skimmer. She's fast and fresh."

In a matter of minutes a line of men went out from the home ranch on a fast lope. All the Fingermarks were under them but old Thunderfoot and Stormwind, along with the best of the always-waiting remuda, and Ann stood listening to them go with a strange, cold weight upon her heart.

Little Fawn came from the kitchen and stood silently beside her. "No good," she said presently, "somethin' no dam' good this night."

"What you mean?" the girl asked fearfully.

"Not know what mean," the brown woman said profoundly. "But just not good."

And before they had gone a mile the men of the Double

K knew also that it was not good. They knew stampede had
started, and such a stampede as none of them had ever
witnessed, too monstrous to be estimated, too overpower-
ing to be stemmed. Four thousand, six thousand, eight
thousand head, maybe, of running cattle headed east toward Abilene! A planned, controlled stampede, as much
as any such tide, once set flowing, could be controlled. This
they knew with complete finality by the sounds of shots
which now were cutting through the rolling billows of the
bawling, the age-old method of the rustler to scare and start
the quiet stock. They needed nothing more to tell them
that the Kincaid herds were being swept off Kincaid range,
and there were three among them, Sloan and Bryce and
Starbuck, besides Big Red himself, whose memories flashed
back with chilling knowledge of other herds, in other years,
swept off these very plains toward Abilene. The Jount boys'
herds, from the Jount boys' land; others from over west,
from north.

The pendulum had swung so many years ago, toward
Big Red and his mounting wealth. Now it was swinging
back toward his undoing.

Three miles north and west of home ranch they met the
horror of this thing. In the starlit darkness of the summer
night the whole earth seemed to move. The big gray blanket which the Daunces had brought up from the Llano
Estacado was four times its size, black in the dim light, not
creeping now but flowing like a flood across the land. And
all along its southern edge those many riders raced, shooting into the air, yelling constantly in a wild staccato pitch.
They knew the Double K would come up from south, and
they were ready for them.

The Double K was ready, too. No man among them
but knew the thing was hopeless, that nothing living could
stop that moving tide until it had run itself to exhaustion,
and by then it would be so far away, the coming fight so
far behind, either one way or the other, that there would

be nothing left to do. Knowing this, every man of the Kincaid outfit went into action, the hair-trigger action of the time and place and circumstance.

Outnumbered two to one by the farseeing provision of Frank Daunce, to whom this was ancient business, they began to race and shoot. Wherever a gun flashed its streak of light, there another sought its target. Reckless, owing nothing to Big Red beyond his fabulous wages, yet bound to him and his by the peculiar tie that was common among them, they headed into this swift inferno without a moment's hesitation. These were Double K cattle and they were Double K men, and that was sufficient. Oath and scream and plunging mount, flowing with the stampede toward the east, they fought it out as men of the far frontiers have fought out such things since a single cow-brute grazed the great grasslands. Horses were hit and stumbled, fell, rolled kicking on the earth, their riders flung apart from them to catapult to safety or to be ground to rags beneath the thundering hoofs. No one knew where the other was, each fought as best he could, flaming with vicarious fury, offering his own life in defense of cattle which did not even belong to him, after the fashion of their kind.

It was a losing game, a foregone battle. The billowing black blanket swept on. One by one the riders fell back along its flanks, still shooting, and finally the monstrous drag, a full mile wide, drew up abreast, passed on, began to vanish into that oblivion which was its aim and end. Defeated, scattered, the Kincaid men sat their panting horses in the quieting dark and drew deep draughts of air into their laboring lungs. Then presently Ennis Sloan, bleeding from a shoulder wound, stood in his stirrups on Flyer and began to call into the tragic night.

"Red!" he cried loudly. "Red! Where are you, Red?" There was no answer, and he began to call his men. "Spink! Farloe! Harris!"

"Here!" someone called from far over east, and, "Here!

Here!" the voices came eerily down the trampled line. Harris, Fisher, Farloe rode up to him, but Bryce and Starbuck did not answer, nor did Big Red.

It was odd that no one thought of Ben Alverson.

"It will be moon-up in another hour," Sloan said sharply. "Until then get off your horses and hunt on foot."

It was slow business and brought them little knowledge. Here and there darker humps in the darkness proved trampled cattle—the weak, the old, the very young—and they found two horses dead, their riders nowhere near. But finally the big round moon came up, late and at the full, and they began to find the calm night's tragic toll.

Two flattened things that had once been men, a Mexican and a long blond boy, and Breezy. Beautiful Breezy, still and trampled, her blue eyes still open, but very peaceful now, the ramping wildness done for. They found old Sunbolt too, as still, as·peaceful. But of the men who'd ridden them, Spink and Starbuck, there was no trace.

And as the moon's light grew and brightened they came upon the keynote of the whole sad business, that one for whom the pendulum was swinging after so many wildfire years, Big Red Kincaid, sitting cross-legged upon the earth, his white face blank above his beard, staring into nothingness. Before him lay Ben Alverson. Or what had been Ben Alverson so short a time ago.

"Oh, God!" Ennis Sloan said softly. And Big Red began to talk.

"Got him," he said loudly. "Two of 'em come at me. They was shootin' high, account of Streaker. They wanted her. I heard one yell to look out for her. But Ben—he was a little way ahead—he come a-boilin' back an' rode right in between me an' them. Dam' if he didn't! He was my friend. They drilled him from both sides to once, but he reached an' knocked me clear of th' saddle an' we both come down together. That was th' last I saw. They hazed th' mares away."

He stopped and sat once more like a staring idol.

And in the strained silence the moonlight picked out the silver wings along the dead man's temples. He had failed in what he wanted most of life, namely the love of a young girl, but in that failure he had set himself forever in her heart. Never, so long as she lived, would Copper Ann Kincaid forget Ben Alverson, or that first kiss he had ravished from her lips. And least of all would she forget the words of that last promise, given half banteringly, "Don't fret. I'll go along to keep the old boy out of trouble." Literally, and to the final letter, he kept that promise.

By dawn every rider of the Double K had straggled in, and in every case they were on foot. Bryce and Starbuck both were wounded but able to walk. They told the same story as the rest—shot at, shooting themselves until their guns were empty, then roughly shouldered out of saddle by two men, one on either side, their horses taken. In every case too, it was the horses which had saved them from death. The wonderful, flying, flashing horses of the Fingermarks, which the raiders were so careful not to hurt. The horses which were gone.

There was left only Flyer under Sloan; Hotwind and Bluefire under Harris and Fisher. Farloe rode a common horse. Breezy was dead. Sunbolt was dead. Streaker, the great mare, was gone, and so was Skimmer who had been under Alverson, and Cyclone under Bryce.

The priceless treasures of the Double K had vanished in the night.

The wild, flighty, lovely things, the barren beauties who could not reproduce themselves, the horses of the Fingermarks. Five of them were lost forever. Back at home there were only Stormwind, the peak and pinnacle of them all, however; and Thunderfoot, the matriarch, too old to ever breed again.

Perhaps six thousand head of prime longhorns had vanished with them.

There was no use to follow, to try to prove ownership in
Abilene. There were too many riders on the herd's drag. It
would only mean more death. And every man of the
Double K knew of those secret markets at railhead where
all brands flowed hurriedly toward the distant east and no
questions asked, where spurious bills of sale with forged
signatures were flourished, such matters quickly closed.

They should have known. In all conscience they should
have known—Big Red and those of his riders who had been
with him longest. Perhaps they thought of the Jount boys
now.

And Boss Kincaid, the tycoon, the cattle king, the ruthless gatherer of wealth, the man of might and power, sat
on the trampled earth where all these things had passed
and stared, unseeing, at the coming dawn.

Ben Alverson was buried in the little cemetery, close by
that still new mound that covered poor Bill Smith, and
the town was very quiet.

Behind both graves, directly and indirectly, they saw
the shadowy figure of Big Red Kincaid, and the slow anger
that had grown within these people for many years bulged
and spread with sudden, mushroom growth.

Two watchers in the silent groups that day went deeper
than the sullen anger. Velantry, pale beneath his dusky
skin, was sorry to his foundations that something which he,
himself, had started had cost this man his life, even though
Alverson had chosen to take sides against him, elected to
stand with the Kincaid fortunes. Stella Adams, watching
from the willows' fringe, sensed the rage against Big Red
and hated them all because of it.

But the fire, lighted in Velantry with the first knowledge
that Kincaid was that mythical figure of the hidden scar,
the great stature, the wild red beard which he had hunted
for so long, was burning fiercely now.

Part of that task which he had set himself was finished.

Two parts, in fact, the first and second phases. Big Red knew who he was and what he knew by his taunt of those two names flung at him some time back. Big Red had lost the greater part of that vast wealth which he had built up over blood and tears and wrong throughout the years.

There remained the third and final phase—the phase of Big Red's death which alone, in Velantry's mind, could even up the score as much as such a score could be evened. But over and behind and through the flame of passion in him there appeared a thing he did not wish to see, something which dragged against his spirit as an anchor drags a drowning man. Close his mind against it as he would, it was ever present with him. By day and darkness it was there, breaking now and again the steadiness of his hands, starting the sweat upon his temples. It was the proud, courageous figure, the shining head, the long blue eyes of Copper Ann Kincaid. When he could no longer bear the shadowy image he would take the Ringer and go for those long and solitary rides, sunk in his bitter thoughts.

And so the threads kept drawing in toward their final knot, when the purpose of his life would be fulfilled. Live or die himself, it would be fulfilled.

Out at the Double K the girl with the long blue eyes wept drearily in the solitude of her own room. She wept honestly and sincerely for Ben Alverson, set him on that pedestal of immortal memory in her heart which he could in no other wise have occupied. She wept for the wild young creatures with the cream and silver crests who would never race the open range again. And she wept for Red Kincaid; Red Kincaid, whose face was half mad with some inner fear and fury which she could not know, whose hairy killer's hands picked constantly at his garments.

Chapter Fourteen

ON A DAY OF HIGH BLUE SKIES AND SMALL SOFT WINDS THE man behind this bitter situation rode cautiously along the Bent Bow Creek far over west. He was on Kincaid range, and he kept to the fringe of willows and his black eyes searched the vast expanse of plain and scrub and bunch grass spread out before him. There was in him a cold, grim sense of satisfaction, for where before those rolling plains had been dotted thick with grazing cattle, they were almost empty now.

The Daunce boys had done their work to a very great perfection.

He sat quietly on Ringer with his hands upon the pommel, and he did not know that this quiet scene was charged with tragedy. But so it was, for Red Kincaid, cautious too, drawn by that same desire to see the extent of his ruin, was riding west on Stormwind, threading the cottonwoods along a dry wash at the north. And a mile behind him his daughter followed on Bluefire, her young face drawn and anxious, fearing what she did not know.

That Big Red was an engine of destruction now she knew very well, but whether against the world or against himself she had no way of knowing. He spoke to no one at the Double K unless he had to. He had taken Stormwind, who was Ann's own property, given to her outright long ago, without a by-your-leave, and set him in lost Streaker's place as his own mount. That something was building up inside the half-mad man the girl was sure, something sinister and iron-hard, and she was filled with such fear as she had never known. She wondered pitifully if this was the thing that Jenny had felt those last few years of her life, when she had cried and lost the will to live, this fear of the unknown man that was Big Red beneath his laughter and his boasts—this strange, violent, beastlike man.

Ann shivered as with cold in the drowsy summer day and peered ahead into the empty distance. Red and Stormy were out of sight, but she followed with a powerful inner urge that she could not resist. Wherever Big Red went, whatever he did, she must be there, behind him. And so she rode carefully, holding Bluefire down to a fretting trot, listening with all her sharp young senses. She kept well into the cottonwoods, too, skirting the wash with a furtive feeling of secrecy that was new to her. What did she fear? Was it Big Red himself, the man he had become? Was she afraid of her own father and for her own safety? She did not know. He carried a rifle now, slung ready across his saddle bow, the six gun that always rode his thigh discarded for this deadlier weapon. Surely the world had changed and darkened, and she was lost and frightened.

She came to the place where the Bent Bow made its graceful turn toward the north and west and the dry wash turned also, leaving a wide, deep strip of plain between, and it was there, just at the curve, that she heard the shot. One shot, clear and clean in the summer stillness, and her heart seemed to stop. She held her breath and listened but there was nothing more. Just that one report, far off and dead ahead. Bluefire heard it, too, and stood high on his striped hoofs, his blue eyes wide, his nostrils spread. Like horse and rider carved in stone the young things stood and waited. To save her life Ann could not move, could not urge him forward. What had that one shot meant? Had Big Red killed himself? She opened her mouth for the breath that seemed denied her, and the quiet prairie swam before her vision.

Five—ten minutes passed like those awful moments in a nightmare when one strives to move and cannot, and then she heard a sound in the stillness. It was the long roll of Stormwind's running feet on the drum-head of the earth,

Stormwind coming at full stretch, and above that lovely syncopation there was the sound of laughter. Vast, gargantuan laughter, Homeric in its volume, wild, completely mad, triumphant; and sweeping down toward her she saw the man who made it. Big Red, standing straight up in his stirrups, riding like an acrobat, the rifle held in his right hand high above his head, shouting with unholy joy.

Two hundred yards away they passed her like a grand but monstrous apparition and thundered on toward the home ranch, and for the first time in her life this girl cowered down in terror. When they were gone she slowly roused and touched Bluefire's mane, moved out of the cottonwoods. There was in her a beating tide of smothering emotions, fear and relief and the tightening of some awful premonition.

So it was not himself Big Red had killed.

But he had killed. She knew that with a terrible finality. Only an act so monstrous could produce in him so unspeakable a state of triumph, could unleash the hidden fires of wickedness that had lain so deeply covered through the pleasant years. And as her reason traced his course the palms of her hands began to sweat, for she knew despairingly where that course would end, what she would find somewhere ahead. There was a coldness at her heart, the summer world still swung drunkenly before her eyes, but she did not turn back. The courage that was in her steadied her now as she put the stallion to a run. She swung into the open and raced toward the west almost in Stormwind's tracks, searching desperately each yard of the rolling land, but there was nothing in sight except the scattered longhorns grazing.

When she had gone as far as she thought Big Red had been when he fired that shot, she stopped and looked and listened, holding her breath. But there was only the silence and the sunlit plain. She turned Bluefire and headed for the willowed creek toward the south. Here there were clumps of sumac and tall mullein and the nameless weeds that seek the damper ground, and she threaded in among them, bending from her saddle to search each shadowed spot. Suddenly, without warning, just by a dogwood bush whose white blooms had shattered down, she came upon the thing she'd feared to find.

A man. The sprawled figure of a man in a good black coat, lying face down in the stillness. His wide hat had fallen off, and a scattering of sun came down between the lacy leaves to set a shine and sparkle on the blackness of his hair. Even lying so there was a grace about his lean young form, a nonchalance in the hand with its long gambler's fingers flung out across the earth. A slow red trickle moved from under him.

In one helplessly flowing motion Copper Ann Kincaid slid from Bluefire's back to her feet, to her knees, to that lowest of all human levels, the height of a man lying dead upon the sod. As if she could not help it, as indeed she could not, she bowed above him, her forehead on his temple, her lips against his cheek.

"Johnny!" she cried, in a frankly breaking voice. "Johnny Velantry! Oh, my Heaven!" And she began to weep in long hard sobs that wracked her where she lay.

To this girl, who had seen her whole world slide from under her because of this very man, it seemed the end had come. Pride, wealth, and way of life—they seemed in this black moment to have lost their meaning. Only this man, this black-haired man with the somber eyes, who had all but broken her across a gaming table, in the circle of whose arm she had hung one heady moment, seemed now to be the end and aim for which her whole existence had been formed. She knew that now with certainty. Now, when the knowledge came too late. Now, when he lay dead.

How long she lay there, the tears from her own face bathing his, she did not know, but presently she moved, slipped her arm beneath his head, and rolled his body over

to hold him up against her breast. Across his right temple
just above the ear a long red furrow dripped monotonously.

Dripped! That blood was flowing!

Then the heart—the heart—perhaps the heart was beating!

Gently she laid him down upon his back, tore back the
bloodstained coat, the shirt. She bared his breast and bending close, pressed her ear hard on it, listening as she'd never
listened in her life, with every nerve there was in her. Slow,
faint, uneven, missing a beat but going on again, she heard
it, the most blessed sound in all the world, the sound of a
living heart.

John Velantry was alive. Death had missed him less than
a quarter of an inch, but it had missed. That rifle, aimed
expertly for a man's head, had hit its mark, but just a bit
off center, just a trifle wide—and all the Homeric laughter,
the half-mad triumph which had ridden down the wind
toward home, was empty as that wind itself!

Big Red had shot Velantry, had seen him fall, had perhaps looked down upon him with all his old arrogance, his
cruelty, had let him lie for the vultures to find, and ridden
off in triumph. Back across his ravished range, that could
be restocked again! Back to the power he had lost, that
could be rebuilt by such a man as he! And back to ultimate
and final safety. It was no wonder that the tycoon laughed.
No wonder that he rode the racing stallion standing in his
stirrups. No wonder that he held aloft the symbol of his
long years' prowess, the gun still faintly smoking.

But the fate he thought he'd conquered must have
flown above him, laughing too, for behind him in that
lonely thicket his daughter tore a fine white shirt and made
a bandage to stop a bleeding wound.

Johnny Velantry lay still and white beneath the dogwood
tree, and Ann Kincaid knelt beside him, her eyes, burned
dry of tears by terrible anxiety, fixed on his face in the soul-
deep look which a good woman bends upon the man she

loves. Her mouth was open and all the color drained from her golden skin as if she, too, bled, but inwardly.

She rolled the blood-wet coat to make a pillow, and as she did so something slipped from an inside pocket to fall against her knee. It, too, was wet, a soggy thing of soft black leather, so worn that it was limp and fragile. It opened as it fell, its contents spilling. She pushed it aside, intent on raising that helpless head, watching the bandage where the spreading stain was creeping, but more slowly now. Not for nothing had Copper Ann been raised in the fashion of the frontier where harsh things happened often and everyone must have the knowledge to combat them. She had made an expert dressing, binding a roll of cloth hard down upon that long red furrow, and now she watched its working. The man was still unconscious but the flow of blood was stopping.

And Copper Ann looked down upon that precious packet which had shaped Velantry's life, would shape her own. She saw two faces there, the dark and laughing girl, the thin blond man. A man in a striped coat! A man with Velantry's eyes, his handsome temples, the unmistakable, winged brows! Why, this was the face of John Velantry himself, though fair instead of dark! She looked from the one to the other in sudden understanding. Two on the same pattern—one a little older than the other—both with the sensitive, suffering mouth, the somber eyes.

Father and son! This man in the stripes of shame, the felon's clothes, was—must be—Velantry's father. The dark girl had to be his mother. Looking painfully upon these things Ann closed her open lips, swallowed the lump that was growing in her throat.

So. This was the key to all Velantry's hardness, his solitary life, his bitterness. Here was the reason why he kept apart from women, from love itself. Why he had drawn so sharply up that day on Ringer's back when his face had bent so near her own, his lips seemed forming helplessly for a kiss. Why he had so rudely dropped her in the dust, given back to her her own contemptuous words, "scrub stock."

This man was set aside. This man would not love, nor let himself be loved—not with that heritage behind him. With the quickness which was so great a part of her she saw these things. But there was a gap in her reasoning, an ominous hiatus which she could not fill.

Where did Big Red come in?

Why had Velantry set himself against him and all things pertaining to him, so coldly, so completely? Against his standing in the country; against his wealth—she thought of that day in the Lone Star Palace when this man had tried to break the Double K, and probably would have done so had it not been for Curly Bates—against herself as Big Red's daughter? There was something evil here, something sinister. She remembered Big Red's change of late and wondered, though she had nothing to go on there since she had not been present when Velantry flung those two names at him, and no one had told her of the incident. No one at the Double K told Copper Ann unhappy things. Now she was discovering them for herself. Slowly and painfully, groping through mysterious shadows, she was seeing the tycoon as he was and the sight was terrifying.

This man in the convict's stripes with the suffering eyes, what did he mean? She picked up the packet and studied the pictured face. It was a gentle face, clear and straightforward, with no trace of shame upon it, though it bore the stamp of utter resignation, utter hopelessness.

And then she saw the folded letter tucked in behind the photograph.

Instantly a light broke in upon her. Here was the answer, she felt with sharp certainty. Here lay the explanation to all that had happened since the early spring. She sat still upon her knees, holding this vital knowledge in her hands, shaken with fear and sorrow, searching her heart for the right.

This was Velantry's property, his secret, most intimate possession, that she knew. It was sacrilege to look upon it. Yet what might she not do with it? What further bloodshed might she avert? What pressure might she not bring to bear if she stepped in between these two deadly men, armed with their knowledge and their purposes?

This reasoning was clear to her and, in sober faith that it was right, she drew the letter out and opened it. It lay in her trembling hands, thin and worn as though from many readings, its creases almost broken, and it was dated Fairbanks, Alaska, more than four years back.

To JOHN VELANTRY HOLT, it read, INDEPENDENCE, MISSOURI.

My dear Nephew: This letter is by way of being my last Will and Testament, as the doctor here says I have not long to live. Lung trouble. That is too bad, since I had further plans for my life. But a man must take what comes, especially when his health is gone. And so my plan is lost to me, personally, though I hope it will be carried out to its last minutest detail by you, who are the very last of our blood on the Holt side. I don't know much about your mother's people, or if any of them are living. Poor woman, she was good and pretty, and she died early. If ever a woman died of a broken heart, she did. Just grieved herself to death. Your father, William Henry Holt, my only brother, had died the fall before. Of course you remember both of them, for you were about seven years old at the time. You probably remember me, too, since it was I who took you away and put you in boys' school in New York state. And you've had letters from me from time to time, though I was always a poor writer of letters. I kept you in school until you were eighteen. Then you went on your own with the money I had placed in escrow for you.

Since then, as you know, you have not heard from me often, though I've kept track of you. And I may say here that you have done all right with your life so far and with your education, which has been good. But now I mean to change all that, if you're the man I think you are. You are now between twenty-two and twenty-three years old, a man if you'll ever be. I feel you are ready to take over the thing I've meant to do, but which I've been too busy making money up here to get around to. First, I have put at your disposal, and in your name, the bulk of my fortune in the First National Bank there at home. You are to show them the personal note I shall enclose with this, bearing my signature, which they have on record there. I mean for you to use this money as I would have used it—namely, to track down and find a man. A big man, a huge figure of a man, with red hair and bright blue eyes and a lot of laughter in him. His name is—or was, perhaps he's changed it long ago—Martin P. Concannon.

Twenty years ago your father was head teller in that very bank. Concannon was his assistant. They worked together and were friends, and both stood pretty high with the officials of the bank. Your father was a little older. He was married and had you. Concannon had not married yet; he did soon after. To make a long story short—I get pretty tired trying to write, even bringing all this back to mind— well, there came a day when suddenly, right out of a clear sky, there was a terrible trouble at the bank. A great shortage in your father's department—money gone overnight, lots of it,—and of course he was the logical suspect. There was an investigation. William was aghast, for he could not account for it. Things had been all right one day, the next this. He protested his innocence, but he was indicted and went to trial and was convicted. And the only witness against him was his assistant, Martin Concannon. He was the cleverest witness I ever heard take the stand—hesitant, reluctant, as if it hurt him to even mention the damning things he said he'd been noticing about William. How he'd been preoccupied for weeks, thinking, nervous; how Concannon had had to do some of his work for him, and so on. All this went over big with the jury and when the time for decision came William was convicted and sentenced to life imprisonment. Your mother fainted that day in the courtroom, and I got into trouble myself for I tried to kill that lying, smug, cocksure man whose testimony had brought that verdict. I jumped him as your father was led away, tried to cut out his heart, but all I did was carve a deep half-circle on his left breast because a guard grabbed me.

But I left my mark on him, a mark he'll wear to his dying day, for it went rib-deep. I saw it as they tore his clothes off, right there in the courtroom. They clapped me in jail, and it was months before I got free of the law. By that time William had begun his sentence in the penitentiary—and Martin Concannon had left the country. They said of him that the testimony he'd been forced to give had broken his heart, so he gave up his position and went way. But that money, all that considerable amount, was never found. The papers figured William had hidden it somewhere. Detectives watched your mother for a year. But neither she nor William lived long to suffer from this wreck of their innocent lives. William died ten months after entering prison; she followed the next fall. I've kept their pictures for you all this time, meaning to bring them when I came to do the job I started in that courtroom. But now I'll never do it. Should have, long back, but you know—or you will know as you get older—how easy it is to put things off.

And so I've drifted beyond the possibility of that vengeance which I swore to take on Martin Concannon that long past day. That is, personally. Maybe I'll do it yet, through you. For I'm laying the job on your shoulders, John. Whatever you are doing, drop it. There'll be no need for you to earn money. You'll have enough for life if you take care of it. But I hope you'll take up the task I should

have done and finish it. Look at the two faces in these
pictures. Your mother—young, happy, with a right to the
best in life, but dead of grief before her time. Your father
—in a convict's stripes, dead too. Now you take up the job,
young John. Hunt down all red-haired men, big men with
blue eyes who laugh a lot. Investigate their backgrounds,
where they came from—when, if they have money. But
before you do anything be sure, be certain sure, that your
man has a half-moon scar just over his heart, a perfect half
circle with the points turned down. When you find him
speak two names to him and watch his face. Speak of
William Henry Holt and Martin P. Concannon. If it is
your man he should get a shock that will show on his face.
Once you are sure, I want you to do these things—for me,
for your mother, for your father. Most of all for that good
and decent man who was made the scapegoat that a black-
hearted scoundrel might go free. Free to enjoy that stolen
wealth. All right. Find him. And break him. Someway,
somehow, I want you to break him first of all. Sweep away
his wealth. Break his pride. Then put into him fear. Those
two names will do it. And when you've done all this, then
kill him, Johnny, as I meant to do. Kill him if you've got
the guts.

And now I'm very tired. I'll say good-bye. And I'll ask you
to forgive me for laying on you so tremendous a job—the
job I failed at myself.

Very truly yours, JOHN SAMUEL HOLT.

P.S. You see you are my namesake.

With fingers that were ice cold but very steady, Ann
Kincaid carefully folded this tragic and remarkable docu-
ment back in its worn creases and slipped it in behind the
photograph where it had been before. She closed the packet,
wiped its outside with a handful of leaves, and returned it
to the pocket of the coat, moving the inert head to do so.
Whatever happened, if Velantry lived, he must not know

what she had done. But there was in her no self-condemnation for her act. It was right that she should have read that record, that she should know its contents, for now she had the answer to everything she had not understood. A sad and awful answer to everything she had ever asked of Little Fawn, to all the mysterious doings of the Double K throughout the years. She knew for sure and certain now what manner of monster Big Red was. Big Red whom she had loved so much, whom Jenny had once loved, and whom both had come to really know at last. Big Red Kincaid—traitor, thief, killer. Not only had he killed with laughter and his smoking guns—the Jount boys, Bill Smith, Velantry now—but he had killed the souls of those two back in Missouri, had killed the soul of Jenny.

His daughter did not weep now. She was calm and dry of tears, filled with a great pity. Pity for those strangers in a land she did not know, pity for her own mother, even pity for Big Red himself that he could be so lost. Eternally lost, facing his own death someday with these dark things on his soul.

And pity for this man lying so still before her. This young man who had taken on that somber task, literally and with all his heart. This Johnny Velantry who might die, too, who might never see the golden summer light again.

As a mother bends above her stricken child, but as a woman holds her man, Copper Ann bent down and lifted Johnny's face against her own, kissed him gently on the lips. As if that touch were like a draught of life, a shining cord to hold him back against the darkness which encompassed him, he stirred and breathed more deeply.

"Johnny!" the girl whispered. "Oh, Johnny!"

When the blackness of utter oblivion began to give way to returning consciousness, it seemed to Velantry that he struggled upward through deep waters. The light came back to him dimly, exactly as it does through the dark depths of the sea, and he felt a great gratitude for just that common but miraculous thing, the light of day. He moved and tried to lift his head, but with that effort the light went out at once and he sank down again. But the girl raised him higher against her own body, leaned back to hold him so, and presently he moved again, his eyes partly opened. They stared dully at the green cloth of her riding habit, with no recognition in them, and she held her breath, waiting. Presently she bent her face into that unfocused line of vision and whispered his name.

"Johnny," she said softly. "Johnny Velantry."

The sound of her voice in the stillness that had encompassed him broke through the deadlock of his senses, and consciousness came fully back upon his face. He looked up at her wildly, remembering something.

"You!" he said. "You shot me! It was a shot. I heard it before I fell off Ringer! Before the light went out!"

Ann's face broke into the pattern of fresh agony and she began to cry again. "No, no!" she wailed. "Oh, no! I didn't! I didn't! Oh, Johnny, believe me! Please believe me! Would I try to kill you if I—if I feel like this toward you? See." She drew him back against her breast and laid her shaking lips on his and kissed him profoundly. "I've been in love with you since the first time I laid eyes on you, I think. I did not want to be. I hated you—for your enmity, and your indifference, your hard and bitter words——"

Here the memory of that stark new knowledge which she possessed stood forth in her conscience like an accusing figure, and she cried more terribly, accepting that accusation against her blood, its justification.

"I love you," she said brokenly. "I will always love you, for I've loved no other man. I shall never love another man."

"Stop!" Velantry cried harshly. "Don't say it! You must not!"

He tried to move away from her, from the danger of her

soft young arms, her tear-wet, grieving face, but the world swung in its orbit wildly and he closed his eyes again.

"Why?" she said. "Oh, Johnny, why?"

It seemed to her as if she and all her life belonged to this man forever. All that she could ever do, all the love she could ever give him, could not wipe out a jot or tittle of the wrong her blood had done him, but all that she was, would ever be, belonged to him. Deep in her heart she knew this was so, that nothing could ever change it.

"Why?" she whispered humbly, her pride, the flaunting Kincaid pride, dissolved like vapor in the white heat of this dreadful crisis.

John Velantry rolled from her knees and lay face down among the dogwood blooms once more. "Because," he said, "it can't be. Not if we were the last two persons on the earth! Go away. Now! Now while I'm still able——"

"Able for what, Johnny?" Ann pleaded softly. "Able for what?"

The man rolled back and looked up at her with his black eyes full of light. "To let you go!" he gritted. "To see you ride out of my life and never look on your face again! Is that what you wanted to hear, Copper Ann Kincaid? To know you've added one more victim to your string?"

Harsh as he tried to make the words, as wounding, they struck no fire from the tender face above him, a face that in this hour was all Jenny's—loving, gentle, faithful to whatever end the dedication of her love might lead. For Jenny it had led to heartbreak and an early death. For her daughter it might do the same.

Long Velantry looked up at the drowned blue eyes, the pale lips that had kissed him, and the foundations of his life broke under him.

"Ann," he said sadly. "Oh, Ann—Copper Ann—forgive me." He turned his face against her breast and put his arm around her. "I, too," he said, "from that first day in the

Lone Star. I've fought the thought of you every day, every hour, every restless night. I've ridden miles upon miles trying to get you out of my blood, out of my vision. You have made me weak when I should have been strong—and I did not dare to love you."

"But you do," the girl said simply. "It was meant to be. I've known men all my life and never one I wanted, until I looked up that day and saw your face. You'll never get me out of your blood, out of your vision. We must go on from here together, Johnny. There is no other way."

She was thinking more deeply than he knew, making that pledge to life which Big Red himself had laid upon her even before she had been born. Kincaid blood—Concannon blood, how strange it sounded!—owed more to John Velantry Holt—that, too, was strange—than it could ever pay, but all she would ask of life was the chance to try.

So she looked down and the man looked up and the love between them, born of hate and wrong and vengeance, was, in spite of all, a shining thing. There was sorrow in it, and potential death, for both of them knew that the shot which had struck Velantry this day would not be the last, and that the future was dark with portent. But there was beauty in it, too, and courage, and resignation to the price it might exact. To Velantry there was more than that. There was treason. If he accepted this girl it could not be across Big Red's dead body. If he let him live he, Velantry, would be a traitor. A traitor to the man in the convict's stripes, to the young wife who had followed him in death, and to that other John Holt who had laid upon him the bitter task of vengeance.

With his face against Ann's shoulder Velantry passionately wished that that ambushed marksman had done a better job. It would have been better all around, have solved all mysteries, paid all scores—and he would not have been called upon to make so unspeakable a sacrifice, both ways. If only he could think more clearly! If the world did not spin and sink so when he tried to move! If the feel, the strength, the beauty of this girl were not about, beneath, above him, in arms and breast and tender face! If only——

He shook his bandaged head and closed his tired eyes and was lost. That minute he was lost, though he did not know it yet. It took her gentle lips' again on his own to rouse him from the mists and stupors that seemed drifting in again, and her urgent voice filled with anxiety to hold him to consciousness.

"Johnny," she was saying desperately. "Oh, Johnny, wake up! Please wake up. Try. Try hard. You've got to try."

She lifted him to a sitting posture, and though the earth rolled under him, he managed to hold it.

"Do you think you can stand up?" she begged. "If I hold you? We've got to get to town. We must."

The last words were spoken to herself more than to him, for her quick mind was working. She wanted no one from the Double K to come hunting for her, least of all Big Red. If Big Red should miss her and come back to this fatal spot —a shudder shook her at the thought.

"Come now, let's try," she urged, and getting to her feet put her arms under his and lifted strongly. With a supreme effort the man came up, to stand and waver dizzily for a time, to steady, and finally to recover balance.

"Oh, fine! Grand!" Ann said. "Now, can you ride? Ringer's just across the creek. If you can't, Bluefire will carry double. Hold to this little tree while I get them."

Velantry managed to mount, but with the first moving out from the dogwood thicket he swung so wildly in his saddle that Ann stopped at once. If he fell he might never rise again, she knew well. So, painfully and laboriously, they made the change and as the long shadows of the prairie twilight began to stretch across the land the big blue stallion stepped carefully under his double burden toward the town.

It was midnight when Sylvester Mead, roused by a knock on his door, stepped out in the darkness to find Ann Kincaid, a shadow among shadows, her voice a whisper.

"Ves," she said sadly. "Come over to the Silver Tip. I've got Johnny on Bluefire. He needs help."

"My God!" Mead said. "What's happened, Ann?"

"Shot," she said lowly.

"Who?"

"Don't ask me, Ves," the girl said miserably.

"I see."

"Just come and help him. Don't rouse the town, please, Ves."

"I'll be right over," Mead said, "just as quick as I get my clothes on."

An hour later Ann Kincaid was nearing the home ranch of the Double K. There were lanterns bobbing across the levels and she could hear the running feet of horses here and there, and she knew the men were hunting for her. Now and then she heard Big Red roaring in the night, blasphemous and violent, blaming the horse she rode, herself, the world at large that she was lost. She could have answered their wild calling but she did not. There was little in her of kindliness or anxiety or allegiance toward these men who had made her life before this night.

Neither was there fear. She rode at a walk and presently someone picked her up in the lantern light, fired two shots in the air to tell the rest that she was found, and she went on toward home in a silence that no one of all those drawing in behind her broke. They knew, these men of the Double K, a crisis when they met it. They knew now that something of vital import had taken place, and that Copper Ann was in it.

Up to the hilt this girl was in it, whatever it was, and they were silent with her silence. As they reached the Big Corral they heard the tycoon coming, riding Stormwind at full stretch, still roaring in his great voice. There were lanterns hung on the gate timbers and their light made a circle of radiance in the dark night, and Ann sat still on Bluefire in that luminous place. She sat still and tall in her saddle, and her face had lost much of its beauty. It was pale and it bore a new hardness. The blue eyes were almost black with the spread pupils.

As Kincaid raced up and slid the stallion spectacularly to a rearing stop they looked at him as if they'd never seen his face before. They were strange eyes in a strange face, not the lovely, laughing orbs of Copper Ann Kincaid, the darling of the place. They were accusing and hard and veiled with a certain withdrawal.

Big Red was his old self again. The self of years ago, dominant, forceful, overbearing, master of his life and of all the other lives which touched it. He was free of fear, safe once more, had been since that hour on the Bent Bow Creek; and he let the whole world know it.

He let his daughter know it now in the roar of anger which poured across her.

"You!" he shouted. "Where you been? Ridin' th' open in th' night like any hussy! You answer me, girl! Where you been?"

For a long moment she did not speak. She sat in the circle of light and looked at him, and no one moved. They saw the untidiness of her shining hair, the soil upon her habit, and something else which stilled even their careful breathing. She did indeed look like some woman of the street, for there was blood, dry and dark, along one shoulder, down her right arm. When she answered it was to shock the still night with her words.

"Martin P. Concannon," she said, "it's none of your damn business."

Chapter Fifteen

BIG RED STRUCK HER THEN, FOR THE FIRST TIME IN HER LIFE, a hard blow with the flat of his hand across the mouth. It almost knocked her from her saddle, but Sloan put out a quick arm and caught her, set her upright. His pale eyes were cold as steel as he looked at his boss.

"Red," he said evenly, "I've been with you a long time. I've seen you do some bad things. We've done some bad things together. But if you ever do that again, I'll kill you sure as shootin'."

Ann slid down from Bluefire. "He'll never do it again, Ennis," she said. "He'll never have the chance."

She walked tiredly up the path toward the house. At the veranda she stopped and turned.

"Keep Bluefire saddled for me, boys," she called. "I'll want him again, soon."

Then she went inside and no one spoke, and the dead silence of the summer night came down. The tycoon sat on Stormwind and what tides of rage and terror surged across his spirit no one there could know.

Martin P. Concannon!

Ann knew that name. Where had she found that knowledge? Only one man in all this country knew its meaning—and he was dead in a dogwood thicket at the bend of Bent Bow Creek. Red knew for sure that he was dead, for he had shot him, had seen him fall, had ridden up and looked at him where he lay in the dappled sun and shade. But a cold hand gripped him now; horror and uncertainty closed down upon his heart. He reined the stallion off and thundered out across the levels in the dark, and his men stood in strained silence listening to Stormwind's long roll on the sounding earth. They did not speak, and no one made a move to put the horses up. They waited for the red-haired girl with that mysterious blood along her sleeve. They had waited for her, most of them, throughout her life, a guerdon of protection thrown around her, a guard of honor precious to each one of them. In this aching silence they felt a sad finality, as if this were to be the last time they would do so.

Inside the dark house Ann stood in her own room and faced Little Fawn across a guttering candle in the woman's hand. The opaque black eyes, unreadable and shallow, were fixed on her pale face.

"What you do?" Fawn asked. "Where you go?"

"Don't know," the girl said straightly. "Only go. From here."

"For always?"

"Yes, for always."

At that a quiver crossed the dark features. "All right," the other said. "You make pack, I make pack. You go, I go."

She set down the candle and moved toward the door, but the girl stopped her.

"No," she said. "No can do. You stay."

Little Fawn stood so, her still face turned toward the dark beyond the open door, and Ann saw a shaking begin across the patient shoulders. She crossed to her and put her arms around her, turned her so that once again she could pillow her tired head on the broad breast where she had found comfort since she could remember.

"Fawn," she said miserably, "I don't know where I go. To town. The Blue Top, maybe. Some day, some place, I'll send for you. You'll be with me always. I promise."

"Promise? Cross?" Little Fawn said dully.

Ann made the little-girl gesture of two strokes across her breast. "Yes," she said. "Cross my heart."

Then she kissed the brown cheek and turned to the saddest task she had ever known, that of emptying this room forever of her presence. She had lived here always. She had no other memories of home.

An hour later she was riding into the after night toward the town, nine men behind her, each carrying some small bundle of her possessions across his saddle bow. They knew that she was leaving the Double K and that all its light and life and beauty was going with her, but no one said a word, no one protested.

There was sorrow here, and mystery, and a heavy grief that showed in her white face, and ruined pride. The great Kincaid pride which had been like a solid stone foundation beneath Big Red and her. It seemed a heap of rubble now beneath them both.

It was gray dawn when they reached the Blue Top Hotel and roused Jonas Biffle. Ennis Sloan lifted his arms and Copper Ann slid into them, looking up at him with the long blue eyes that had been so beautiful. They were wide and haggard now.

"Thank you, Ennis," she said, "for everything. You are a good man."

"My God!" Sloan said. "I wish to Him I was! You let us keep a track of you, Ann. We—we're all behind you. Barrin' nothing, we're behind you."

"I know," she said, "and I will. So long, boys."

Jonas Biffle, astonished and a trifle scared, but ready to face odds, took her in, and the riders turned and went away along the quiet street. Whatever happened further, whatever tragedy was in the offing, they were cattlemen, and there was work to do at the Double K. They had eaten its salt too long to let anything interfere with that, so they headed out toward it in the fresh new day.

In the room at the Blue Top which she always occupied when she stayed overnight in town, Ann slept for six hours like the dead. Then she waked and bathed and dressed herself in one of the neat calicos that Fawn had made for

her, ate the good food Jonas brought to her, and sent for
Sylvester Mead. The storekeeper came with worry on his
face.

"What's this, Ann?" he asked. "Someone saw the men
bring you in. We know Bluefire's in th' stable. What's
happened?"

"Nothing more that matters, Ves," she said. "Only I've
left the ranch because—because Red struck me in the face."

"By damn!" the man said hotly. "You!"

"It's nothing. It was only a straw. The last one."

"I know. Where's Red?"

"I don't know. He left on Stormwind. Ves, how—how
is Johnny?"

"He'll be all right. Still wobbly on his feet. That slug
must have hit him a pretty hard wallop. Funny it didn't
finish th' job. He's cleaned up an' had some breakfast.
Be all right soon."

"Tell him I'm here, Ves. I want to see him."

"He'll be about this afternoon. Chad Shally's comin' in
with th' first load of freight for him an' me. Nobody
molested his wagons since Ben——"

He stopped, embarrassed, thinking of the violent allegiance of Ben Alverson to the Kincaid cause, his death
because of it.

"It's all right, Ves," Ann said gently. "I'm glad. And
I'll be careful. Heaven knows, there's enough talk about
the Kincaids as it is."

There was. The women, from this backyard to that, were
tearing them to pieces. And Stella Adams was worrying.
There was a tightness around her tired and aging heart
that filled her with foreboding. A few times in her checkered life she had felt that stultifying stricture, and always
it had presaged disaster. With profound conviction she
foresaw disaster now. Restlessly she paced the willows by
day, peering at the dusty street, tramped the paths by night.

At two o'clock in the afternoon Ann Kincaid came out of the Blue Top Hotel and mounted Bluefire who stood, fresh and rested, by the rail, his rein in Jonas Biffle's hand. She did not wear the familiar riding habit now, but the simple calico dress, and somehow, with the loss of the handsome habiliment, she seemed to have lost something of Kincaid stature, Kincaid pride. And Bluefire, beautiful as he was, as wild and stamping, was not the great Storm-wind. There was nothing like Stormwind in the whole country, had never been, would never be.

All these things the watching women noted.

"H'm'm," one said, with a certain spiteful relish. "Don't look much like Copper Ann Kincaid, does she? Miss Copper Ann Kincaid, th' darling dream of every male, young or old, this side th' Llano Estacado!"

And she was right. Only the shining, coppery head, the upright carriage of the slender form, were as they had been, and nothing could destroy their beauty. Ann took the rein and rode away along the watching street toward the west. In a few moments she was lost to view where the road wound northwest with the contour of Big Willow Creek, the wagging tongues were left behind.

A little later Johnny Velantry left the town also, going out behind the Silver Tip, the Odeon, the blacksmith shop, and no one saw him go.

For the first time these two were going to a rendezvous whose outcome would set the whole pattern of their lives. The girl was calm and confident beneath her grief, the man tossed on a surging tide of right and wrong, of love and duty, like a ship in a typhoon without a rudder. All day he had fought his battle in his quarters at the Silver Tip, and was still at war with these vital forces. Sylvester Mead had dressed the long wound on his temple, reband-aged it, had seen to it that he ate some heartening food. The swinging world had steadied under him; he was him-self again but for a tremor that ran along his nerves like water over stones each time he thought of the decision he must make, the precepts he must follow.

Avenger or traitor?

Killer or cleanhanded?

Settled, decent, blessed beyond his wildest dream, or a lone wanderer once more with blood on his conscience?

He did not know.

Only when he faced this girl with sober reason and talked the matter out would the issue be settled once and for all.

So he rode to meet her a mile or so away where the cottonwoods grew thick along the stream, and the heart in his breast was laboring with emotions. His face was white with the struggle, his black eyes somber, when he came upon her in a tiny clearing where the sunlight filtered down upon her like a mist of sparkling gold. She, too, was grave of face—a woman with a woman's responsibility heavy upon her. She knew she had not won this man, even though he had confessed his love for her.

"Johnny!" she said softly, when he rode in and pulled the Ringer up beside her. "Oh, Johnny!"

Velantry did not answer. He sat with his hands on his pommel and his gaze fixed on her lovely face where the sorrow he had brought her had left its marks. If he had never seen her, if he had never struck this country, she would still be the laughing, happy girl who had sat that day in the Lone Star Palace and played a game of cards.

Now she was a woman whose whole way of life had changed, whose faith and love in and for an idol had been shattered, whose heritage of wealth had been swept away because he, John Velantry Holt, had talked with the Daunce boys beside a night campfire. He shook his head and sighed and sought for the words he knew he must speak, either one way or the other, and to save his life he could not make the beginning. The decision was beyond him, even now. Now, when he had reviewed it all.

Should he tell this earnest, blue-eyed girl that what he'd

said in the dogwood thicket had been the ravings of delirium? That he did not love her and never would? Should he crush her yet further in the dust that he might ride away to kill her father and even an ancient score of an eye for an eye, a tooth for a tooth?

Or should he take her to his heart and heal, as much as in him lay, the hurt that he had dealt her with all the love of a lifetime together?

Every fiber of him, soul and body, cried out for this decision, ached with longing for her, and yet he sat in silence, his eyes upon her face.

It was Copper Ann herself who broke that silence, who tipped the swinging scales of right and wrong between them. She leaned over and laid her warm hand over both of his upon the saddle bow.

"Don't try, Johnny," she said simply. "Don't punish yourself any more. There is nothing you must tell me. I know it all. I read the letter in the packet; I saw the pictures. I had not meant to tell you, ever, but I know I must. I must make the decision for us both. And I make it now. We'll let the dead past bury its dead and look only to the future. I can never repay the debt which Kincaid blood owes you—nothing can do that. But I can love you till I die. I can spend my life beside you. We can go away together and forget there ever was a wrong behind us, any wrong. I will not let you kill Big Red. Not because he deserves to live, but because you are not a killer yet, and I don't want you ever to be. And we must go at once, or he'll kill you and then—then——" She stopped and wet her lips. "Then, as surely as I live, I would kill him."

She had made her move, had said her say, and Velantry did not move or speak, and this time it was because he could not. There was a choking in his throat, a mist before his eyes. He leaned forward and put his forehead in the curve of her soft shoulder and felt her arms around him.

There was healing in them, and peace, and the washing

away of ancient bitterness. Literally, they smoothed the slate between them, and there was no need for words. The love they bore was like a radiance for the future, oblivion for the past. There was no question now of treason, no obligation for revenge. The innocent man in the felon's stripes, the laughing, dark-eyed girl, they laid no rod upon him, asked no sacrificial blood. In fact, they never had. It was that other John Holt, and as for him, he was long dead among Alaskan snows, beyond all human plans of vengeance.

In the circle of this girl's innocent arms Velantry saw these moving things as in a kaleidoscope. They changed and dropped and fell together, forming the pattern of a new and lovely life, and he seemed to stand among them new himself. Presently he raised his head and looked at her profoundly.

"Yes," he said quietly. "Yes, Ann, we'll go. And we'll go clean."

He leaned and kissed her, and it was a covenant between them.

A little later they came riding back to town together, openly, for all to see, and there was pride about them, and humility, and the calmness of fixed and settled purpose. As they rounded the western turn into the street they saw the Kincaid horses before the Lone Star Palace. Ann's eyes flared and darkened as she counted them. Nine. The men were back in town. Kincaid horses, but they, too, had dwindled in their beauty and their pride for there were only two of the Fingermarks now among the common mounts. Flyer and Hotwind. There was no sign of Stormwind.

Standing about among them, on the Lone Star porch, were the riders of the Double K—still, alert, their eyes covering the street, the buildings that flanked it on either side. There was a tension here. It was apparent in the way they stood, so tense and quiet.

At the Blue Top, Ennis Sloan came down the steps and walked quickly up to Ann. His face was hard and he carried a rifle in his hands. He held it up to her.

"Ann," he said abruptly, "you take this. You may need it. I don't advise you in any way, but you are young and good and you haven't earned any of this. Big Red's on th' loose, and it's our opinion that he's gone stark, raving mad. We don't know where he is, but he rode west on Storm. Ran clean out on us, yelling like an Injun. He'll hit town sooner or later, and he's out for blood. Someone brought him word that—that you're alive, Velantry."

"Thanks, Sloan," Velantry said gravely. "But I'll try to evade the issue. A month—a week ago I wouldn't have, but things are different now. You must see how things are between Ann and me."

"Ennis," Ann broke in swiftly, "we're going. We would have waited till night, maybe—rest the horses, freshen up a little, let Johnny have a little longer. He's still shaky. But we'll go now, this minute. To Abilene. We'll be married there. We——"

She flung up her head like a wild animal listening. The stillness of the street became painful, thin and strained with listening. The whole town was at its fences, on its planked porches, and it stopped its breath to listen. For Ann Kincaid had heard a sound, faint and far off, which she would have recognized a thousand miles away, a thousand years in time. The sound of thunder on the talking plain, the beautiful, wild drumming of shod hoofs, the long roll of a running horse. The unmistakable sign-manual of one horse—the only horse in all the world whose racing feet could thrill her so, even at this tragic moment.

Stormwind! Stormwind the Great! The monstrous blue stallion who was a part of her inmost heart, her pride, her treasure, and her love!

Stormwind was coming in across the prairie at the west

—and she knew he carried death across his saddle bow. For herself, perhaps. Surely and certainly for the man on the tall brown horse beside her.

Ann Kincaid wet her pale lips and looked at Velantry. Then she cried, screaming on a thin, high note, her warning and farewell.

"Go, Johnny! Go!" she screamed. "Full stretch! Run the Ringer out!"

But Velantry shook his head. "Not without you," he said.

Her face broke into agony. "I can't keep up—on Bluefire," she said, "and I'll have to see—see death!"

Sloan looked up at him. "She's right," he said. "It's shooting if you stay. Unless you want it that way?"

"No!" Velantry said. "I don't. Not now. Here, Ann. Proof of my bargain."

He reached beneath his coat and flicked the gun from his left armpit, tossed it to her. It slid from her lap into the dust.

Without a word the man on the brown horse leaned him to the right and went away, and that going was a wonderful thing to see. From a standing start the Ringer seemed to sail up from the earth and out in one long, clean leap. In three jumps he was abreast of the Lone Star Palace and in the clear. Then he was headed east, toward Abilene and that oblivion which had waited for so many things above the Chisholm Trail.

And around the western turn Big Red Kincaid and Stormwind came racing into sight. The stallion was laid out level, running as these watchers had never seen him run, his tail a long bright banner streaming on the wind, his mane a silver smoke above him, his eyes like blue stars in his silver face. The man on his back looked mad in all truth. He rode bent forward, the red shag of his beard and his hair blown back from his madman's face, and he swung his right hand in circles as if he built a lasso loop. In it was his old six gun, a worn and deadly weapon. As he thundered down the open street he saw the rider headed out before him and he struck the stallion's shoulder with the gun, a vicious blow.

It was the first blow of his life and Stormwind seemed to explode with speed. If Ringer, well out ahead, was running magnificently, Stormwind beggared description. He passed the people in the street in one monstrous flash, and they saw him begin to gain on the brown horse incredibly. An audible murmur of exhaled breath went up from them as they visioned what the end must be—for Velantry was unarmed.

This was the race their little world had often talked about, had wished to see, but there had been no horse north of the Llano worthy of the test. There wasn't now. Good as the Ringer was, as young and fast and powerful, he was no match for that monstrous engine coming after him.

They saw that now. And they saw something else.

They saw Ann Kincaid move out behind them on Bluefire and swing into the open beyond the last house, edging north in a widening arc but running parallel. They saw her drop the rein on Bluefire's neck and straighten tall in her saddle, riding magnificently. They saw her raise the rifle. Its crack came clear and clean above the running thunder, and a woman screamed.

Just at the bend of Big Willow Creek they saw the great Stormwind sink and fall, saw him roll down spectacularly in a complete somersault, his four shod hoofs sparkling in the sun above him. And they saw the man on his back sail out far and level to settle, spread-eagled, on his face.

They saw Copper Ann Kincaid fling away the rifle to clutch Bluefire's flailing mane, saw her swaying like a drunkard, almost falling as she passed them. Then she vanished around the bend—she, too, bound for the oblivion that was Abilene.

When she overtook Velantry later on the Chisholm

Trail she was still and white, and she had had her meed of tears.

It was twilight two days later when Sam Bolin tied the tired old pinto before the Stockman's Hotel in the bustling town at railhead and asked for John Velantry. When he found him, spruce and neat in new black clothes, he took off his ancient hat and handed him a letter.

"Be dam', Johnny," he said plaintively, "if you ain't th' runnin'est feller! Two whole days ridin' jest to fetch you this, but Ves Mead he wanted sure fer you to get it—an' he figgered I was th' proper man t' bring it, sence you an' me's pardners, sort of, out at th' Smith place. I hope you give it due consideration," he added anxiously. "Th' hull town does, seems like, th' way they was a-talkin'."

"Well, Sam," Velantry said, "it's good to see you. And, of course, I'll give any word of Ves Mead's consideration. Sit down while I read it."

The letter was short and to the point, but there was no doubt of its sincerity and truth.

Dear Johnny:

I'm sending this by Sam and hope you get it. It's to say we want you to come back, you and Ann. The town does. We had a meeting. So do the Double K men. They don't know what to do, but they're standing by. Because Big Red's gone, bag and baggage, and for good it seems. Stella Adams took him in the best wagon out of Chad Shally's freight string. Paid Chad a monstrous price. Headed southwest across the Llano, bound for beyond the Capitans, she said. She said a funny thing, for the likes of her—something about an honest house and a man comin' in openlike, not among the willers. Tell Ann Red wasn't hurt a bit by his fall, and that Stormy's coming round fine. She just give him an amazing close crease. He's at the stable. And the boys say Little Fawn won't eat, don't hardly sleep either.

Tell Ann. Well, we hope you'll be coming back. The country'll never be the same without you both.

Your friend,

SYLVESTER MEAD.

For a long time Velantry held the letter in his hand and his eyes were far-visioned and very soft. Then he turned and smiled at Sam Bolin, sunk like a heap of dusty rags in one of the lobby chairs.

"Old-timer," he said, "we're going to get you cleaned up and fed and into some new duds, and you can have the town. The whole town. Put the old horse up at the livery stable. Say I'll pay for it. Say I'll pay for anything you may take a fancy to. And I think—I'm sure, if Miss Ann agrees —we'll all ride back together."

"Hell's bells!" the prairie man said testily. "Does it have t' rest with a woman if you come back or not? Wimmen air gettin' so thick out here th' whole country's crawlin' with 'em!"

"Not just a woman, Sam," Velantry said gently, "but Copper Ann. She's Mrs. John Velantry Holt now."

www.ingramcontent.com/pod-product-compliance
Lightning Source LLC
Chambersburg PA
CBHW031127210626
46816CB00015B/1012